M000199782

REVEALING LOVE

SAINTS PROTECTING & INVESTIGATIONS

MARYANN JORDAN

Copyright Revealing Love (Saints Protection & Investigation) 2016

All rights reserved. No part of this book may be reproduced or transmitted in any form or by any means, electronic or mechanical, including photocopying, recording, or by any information storage and retrieval system without the written permission of the author, except where permitted by law.

If you are reading this book and did not purchase it, then you are reading an illegal pirated copy. If you would be concerned about working for no pay, then please respect the author's work! Make sure that you are only reading a copy that has been officially released by the author.

This book is a work of fiction. Names, characters, places, and incidents either are products of the author's imagination or are used fictitiously. Any resemblance to actual persons, living or dead, events, or locales is entirely coincidental.

ISBN ebook: 978-1-947214-20-0

ISBN print: 978-1-947214-21-7

❀ Created with Vellum

(Eighteen months ago)

The backyard party was in full swing and, in typical SEAL fashion, a strange mixture of anything and everything. Some of the men played volleyball off to the side of the yard while others manned the grills. The scent of hamburgers and steaks filled the air. The wives and girlfriends placed the food out onto the tables while some of the married men kept an eye on the kids running around playing. Several of the single men brought dates who stood around nervously looking at the abundance of testosterone. The parties served as a way for the SEALs to unwind in between missions and for friends and families to celebrate and bond.

Jude Stedson came stag, not wanting to bring a girl to one of the group's parties. Most of his pickups were at the bars near the Naval Amphibious Base. Girls flocked there by the droves, prowling and hoping to snag a SEAL—whether for a night or husband hunting. Tall, muscular, with curly, sandy hair only tamable with his military haircut, he was careful to let them know one night with him was all they would get. He had no problem finding beautiful, willing women ready to take just what he offered.

Looking around at the usual crowd, he nodded toward friends and smiled at a few of the single women before walking toward the volleyball game, already jerking his shirt off.

Then she walked in. Beautiful. A girl-next-door kind of beauty that would make every man wish to be her neighbor. Her blue eyes were enormous, set off by her long auburn hair pulled away from her face with a scarf rolled into a headband. Wearing an emerald green sundress held up with little straps, she looked fresh as spring compared to the nameless women from the bars. The dress' tight bodice hugged her breasts before flaring out at her hips and down to just above her knees. As his eyes continued south, they moved from her toned legs down to her pink-tipped toenails encased in little strappy sandals.

He stopped in his tracks, halting the process of pulling his shirt up over his chest, as his eyes locked onto her like a heat-seeking missile. Gazing from the top of her shiny hair down over her luscious body right down to her sandaled feet, he slowly perused back toward her face. Her eyes met his at the same time and he sucked in a gulp of air just to keep standing. Then he looked to her side.

She was on the arm of another SEAL. *Bart something. Taggart. Yeah, Bart Taggart. Jesus, what a lucky bastard to have her on his arm.*

He could not break the bro-code, which meant there was no way he could interfere with another SEAL's date. Determined to see if they were actually dating, or just a pick-up, he moved forward. *She doesn't look like the type for a pick-up, but then Taggart's not exactly known for hanging around the next morning after a fuck either.*

She gazed up at him as he approached and the shy smile on her face caused his chest to clench. Her expression gave him the green light. *Can't hurt to see how attached they are.*

Greeting Bart, he held his breath to see how the girl would be introduced. *If he says "date", then I'll discreetly find out if she's interested. If he says "girlfriend", then I'm screwed.*

As Bart introduced her as his cousin, Jude knew he had won the lottery and hustled to get to her side before any of the other unattached SEALs discovered her availability.

She smiled up at him as Bart made the introductions. *Sabrina. Absolutely fuckin' beautiful name for an absolutely fuckin' beautiful woman.* Jude noticed the pointed stare Bart sent his way, so he returned a quick nod before Bart moved over to others at the party.

"What was that all about?" she asked, looking at the retreating back of her cousin, wondering what secret message had passed between the two.

Jude grinned as he steered her over to the side of the yard so they could talk privately. "What you

3

witnessed was just non-verbal communication between brothers." Seeing the unasked question on her face as she cocked her head to the side, he explained. "He was warning me to treat you like a lady and I was letting him know that was exactly what I was going to do."

Her eyes grew wide as she smiled back. "All that in a look and a nod?"

"Bro-code among SEALs. A language all unto itself."

As she threw her head back in laughter, her long hair swinging down her back, he was sure there was no prettier sound. And for the next six months, between missions, he made sure to hear that sound every day that he could.

(Six Months later)

The hospital bed grew increasingly uncomfortable for him. *Hell, the institutional mattress was past uncomfortable and downright torturous.* Jude knew he should be glad to be alive, but fear his leg injury would keep him from rejoining his SEAL team crept into the corners of his mind. *I've got to get my leg out of this goddamn cast and hope no more surgery is needed. Then I can start the physical therapy that'll get me back to my team.*

His tall, bulky frame made the bed feel minuscule and with his leg in traction, his knee torn to shreds, he could barely move. Running his hand over his closely shorn, sandy hair that he refused to let grow while incapacitated, he sighed heavily.

He tried to think of anything to take his mind off of his discomfort. He thought of his team, each member working in complete unison to complete every mission. Every one of them had visited him, trying to cheer him up, give him hope. But in their eyes he saw the specter of doubt that he might not make it back to them.

Grunting, he turned his mind to his family. His mother visited as well, glad he was alive. She did not want him ever going back to active duty, but knew what this convalescence was costing him.

Then his mind turned to her. Sabrina. *Goddammit, why won't she just go away? She needs a whole man, not someone who doesn't know what the future holds right now!* She had been in to visit earlier and he had given it his best shot. *I was rude, demanding her to leave and telling her to get away from me.* A feeling of guilt shot through him as he remembered the look of hurt followed by determination in her expression.

The four walls began to close in. The four boring walls. He shared the space with three other injured sailors, all recovering from surgeries, waiting to be placed in a semi-private room. Blue walls did nothing to lift his spirits. *Why blue? Do they think it will remind us of calm waters? Fuck that!* The others were asleep but the constant clicks and beeps from the various monitors around the room reverberated in Jude's head, making his already bad mood even worse. *I gotta tell my buddies to bring my iPod and earphones.*

He shifted once more, grimacing as the pain shot

through his leg. He tried not to look at the clock to see how many minutes he had to wait before he could press the wonder-button and receive the morphine drip. Closing his eyes as the pain washed over him, he longed for the ease it would bring. He reached over to call for the nurse when he heard someone enter the room.

His eyes darted over as he heard soft footsteps coming closer. A grimace on his face greeted the visitor. *Oh, great. Just who I don't want to see.* He closed his eyes quickly, hoping the priest would think he was still asleep.

The Naval Chaplain walked into the room, making his early morning rounds of the injured sailors. Jude barely remembered the first visit, when the high doses of pain medicine made everything blurry and hard to focus. During the next two visits, the Chaplain had prayed over Jude, and even though he knew the prayer was for healing and comfort, he felt nothing but discomfort with the priest's presence.

The Chaplain visited each bed in the room, stopping to pray for the injured and recuperating men. Knowing the priest was coming his way, Jude continued to slow his breathing and keep his eyes shut. *Just a little longer and he'll leave.* The soft footsteps came closer.

"I know you are fearful," the Chaplain said, his voice warm.

Fearful? SEALs don't feel fear! Unable to help himself, Jude's eyes jerked open to see the man standing right beside his bed.

"Not afraid of anything, Father," he growled. "I'm just working to get back to where I belong."

"We all belong to God," the kindly man said.

"I belong to my team," he corrected.

He felt the hand of the Chaplain on his good leg and saw him eyeing the leg still in a full cast.

"I understand, but all of the teams belong to God." The priest glanced around, found a chair, and pulled it to his bedside.

Perfect. Just fuckin' perfect. I couldn't keep my goddamn eyes closed and now I get the full attention. Sighing deeply, he schooled his expression. *Might as well let him talk and pray and get it over with.*

"You're determined to re-join your team?" the Chaplain asked.

"Absolutely!" came the fierce answer.

Nodding, the priest smiled. "That's what makes you a good sailor. A good fighter."

Silence ensued as each man quietly took the measure of the other. Jude's leg felt on fire with pain and he wanted to move around, but did not want the priest to see his discomfort.

"You're very courageous," the Chaplain said, his kind expression on Jude.

"I'm a SEAL," he replied, indicating the two were synonymous.

The older man nodded and smiled. "Yes, the two do go together."

More silence.

"But then it sometimes takes more courage to accept what you do not want to face than to rely on old dreams."

At those cryptic words, Jude's brow crinkled in

7

question. "I'm not sure I know what you mean, sir," he replied.

The older man stood and hovered his hand over Jude's cast, careful not to touch it. "We are not always given what we pray for, my son. Sometimes God has other plans to reveal to us. Some people can never accept that and grow. But the truly courageous discover what God has in store for them."

Jude opened his mouth to retort, but no words came out.

"Jude. An Interesting name," the priest commented, a soft smile on his face. "Did you know that Saint Jude was the patron saint of the impossible...lost causes." Continuing to smile, he stood murmuring to himself, "Interesting. Very interesting."

Jude eyed the priest warily. The Chaplain began to pray over him, so he continued to stay silent. As he listened to the words of the priest, he began to sweat. The priest was not praying for healing. Instead, he prayed for Jude to continue to be courageous, no matter where God led him.

He managed to offer a grim smile as the Chaplain left the room. *No way, God. I know You want me to be a SEAL. And that's what I'm gonna keep being.*

(six months later)

It had taken a great deal of perseverance and hard work, but Jude made it from two surgeries to immobile traction, to a wheelchair to crutches, and now to just using a cane. He worked with the physical therapists as often as he could and hit the gym to strengthen his legs. Soon he would be able to get around without the use of the cane. He should be ecstatic...but as he sat on the weight bench, all he could think about was the paperwork sitting in the passenger seat of his truck. Medical discharge. Retirement from the Navy due to medical reasons. *Fuckin' hell.*

Leaving the gym, he was so distracted by the reality crashing down on him, he did not even notice who was standing next to his truck until he was almost upon her.

"Sabrina? What are you doing here?" He knew he sounded like a prick but could not muster the enthusiasm for seeing anyone...*especially not her.* For six months, she had refused to let him crawl into his hole of anger and self-loathing. He wanted her, but would not let her settle for less than what he wanted to be. But she refused to budge. He had been continually rude. Argumentative. Obnoxious. He even made sure one night she saw him leave a bar with another woman. The hurt in her eyes nearly undid him, but he carried through with the charade until leaving the other woman in the parking lot as soon as they exited the bar.

But Sabrina was unyielding in her support of him. And finally they agreed to be just friends. It was all he would give her until he could return to his SEAL team, and now today, with that dream dead—so was his future with her. So friendship would be the only relationship he would have with her. And he knew when she finally met the man of her dreams, it would kill him to watch her with someone else. *But I gotta make the sacrifice...for her.*

His eyes roamed over her of their own volition, the very sight of her warming his heart. She was once again in a sundress, light blue with white polka-dots. Her hair was pulled up in a ponytail and as his eyes drifted from top to bottom, he noted her red toenails. As shitty as his day was, the thought of her little toenails made him grin.

"I wanted to come and be with you. I know today is hard," she replied softly, resting her hand on his arm. "Did you get the paperwork?"

"Yeah," he replied, warring between wanting to jerk his arm away and pulling her into his arms.

They stood in silence. She watched him carefully, looking for a sign of his emotions. Sabrina had waited for so long, knowing Jude was the man for her. It had not been hard, waiting for him, even when he worked so diligently to push her away. *He loves me, I know he does. So I'll just keep waiting until he realizes that I love him...not the SEAL.*

"Come on," she said, giving him a little shoulder bump. "I'll buy you a dinner and if you're a good boy, I'll throw in dessert."

As frustrated as he was, a grin slipped out. *I'm in a shitty mood and she always manages to make me smile.* Wishing life was different so he could be more than a friend to her, he just nodded.

2

(SIX MONTHS LATER - PRESENT DAY)

Jude sat at his desk, staring at his computer. Just staring. The spreadsheets listing the equipment that needed to be ordered, the various bidding paperwork that needed to be submitted, and the piles of files on his desk all began to blur together into one, big clusterfuck of a mess. As a civilian working for the Department of the Navy in logistics, his office was buried inside one of many brick buildings on the Norfolk Naval Base. Like every office on the base, it was a completely bland space. Grey office. Grey furniture. White tile floor. *Boring job. Boring office. Boring...everything!* Unlike those who decorated with family photos, he refused to personalize the space.

He leaned back in his chair, contemplating for the millionth time what he wanted to do with his life. He stretched his left leg, working the stiffness out. The new knee worked well, but the scar tissue running the length of his leg often gave him pain. Running his hand through his curly hair, he sighed deeply. Even now, months later, the desire to pop a few of his pain pills still called to him.

The Navy had been the only thing he ever wanted to do and sitting all day in an office was like being stuck in hell. He had been born to be a SEAL. Proud to be a SEAL. Lived and would have died being a SEAL. He looked around his crowded workspace in disgust. And this job? *So fuckin' not me!*

His teammates, brothers-to-the-end, made sure to include him in everything—parties, events, nights out. *But it's not the same. Not the fuckin' same as being out with them in the field.* And as much as he hated to admit it, he sometimes made excuses so that he did not join them, knowing the pain of not being on the team was worse than the pain of his injury.

His phone rang and for the first time that day, he smiled. Sabrina. The one light in his miserable existence.

Picking up the phone, he answered, "Hey. How'd you know I needed to hear your voice?"

A soft laugh came through the phone and just as always, it hit him right in the gut.

"Well, hey to you too, handsome. Listen, I know you're busy, but I got a call from my cousin and he's coming for a visit. I thought you might like to see Bart again."

He remembered him. The one who had introduced them. A former SEAL. Bart suffered an injury also but left the SEALS voluntarily, even doing some work with Border Patrol. Now he supposedly had some great job, according to Sabrina. *Perfect. I can listen to his glory days and how fuckin' fabulous his life is now. Just fuckin' perfect.*

"Sure, Sabrina," he replied, giving the expected response. While he could not give her what she wanted in their relationship, there was no way he was not going to give in on something that meant so much to her.

"Oh, thank you! I'm sure you and Bart will have a lot to talk about!" she exuded. "And I hate to drop this bomb on you, but you know Nonnie will take this opportunity to get everyone together. But don't stress over it, please. I'll make her keep the gathering simple! You know how she is with family."

Jude knew what she was trying not to say. His own father, a wealthy man, had banged his secretary, promised her the world, then quickly left when she became pregnant. His mom was a loving mother, but growing up it was just him and her since her own parents were deceased. A family that included grandparents, parents, siblings, and extended members? *Completely foreign!*

Before he could get anything else out, the phone disconnected after a hurried goodbye. He sat staring at his cell for a moment, throwing his head back in frustration. *Fuck!*

Nonnie. Sabrina's grandmother, the indomitable Mrs. Arlene Taggart. The woman was old money, with a heart of gold...*and as batty as they came!* She inherited a fortune from her late husband, whose family had been instrumental in the Norfolk shipbuilding industry. When Sabrina's parents were killed a few years ago in a plane crash while on a European vacation, Arlene swooped in to take care of Sabrina. It did not matter that Sabrina was already an adult, Arlene was determined to make up for her parents not being around. She always hinted that she wanted Jude and Sabrina to get married, and he was fairly certain that the subject would come up again at the party.

Leaning forward, he put his head in his hands, elbows on the messy desk.

"Well, don't you just look like the happy camper right now?"

Looking up, he had to smile at Lucy, the administrative assistant providing support to the group of logisticians in the office. "Hello to you too," he greeted, watching her walk over and settle her neatly dressed girth into the seat opposite of him.

Patting her gray hair into place, she eyed him suspiciously. "You, my dear, do not appear to have received good news."

"Oh, it was just a call from Sabrina."

Eyes widening, she quickly responded, "Is everything all right?"

"Yeah, yeah," he assured. "She's got a cousin coming into town and wants me to do the family thing."

Lifting one eyebrow, she repeated, "The *family* thing? Now, Jude, what's so wrong with that? Other than you act like you'd rather have a root canal than hang with her family."

"Maybe I would," he bantered back, only half joking.

Lucy leaned forward, her soulful brown eyes holding his gaze. "I know you hate family events. Lord knows, you've turned down almost every one of my invites."

Chortling, he replied, "Hell, you've got five kids, all married, and how many grandkids? About twelve? Throw in your husband and any distant relatives you can dig up, it's claustrophobic!"

"Humph," she huffed, sitting back in her seat, rolling her eyes. "I only have eleven grandchildren. The twelfth is on the way."

Now it was his turn to roll his eyes. Then a smile settled on his face as he looked at her indulgently. "I know, Lucy. You've always been good to me since I landed this job. You get that my grumpiness is not me, but I don't know what the hell is *me* anymore."

"I understand," she said, sadness coating her words.

From his first days in the office, she had always listened when he would actually talk about what was bothering him. Sometimes, he felt closer to her than he did his own mother.

"So," she said briskly, sitting up straight in her chair. "You've got a fabulous woman—"

"Friend," he interjected. "You know Sabrina is only a friend."

"And that's just because you keep her at arm's length! That girl has stuck by your side through thick and thin and you're crazy if you don't realize that you two belong together."

"Lucy," he warned.

"Fine," she huffed. "But you're just going to have to suck it up and visit with her family. Even if Arlene is getting a little daffy!"

At this, he could not hold the chuckle back. "Yeah. She's a nice woman, but in the last year, she's become so obsessed with trying to speak to her late husband from the great beyond."

"Poor woman," Lucy said, shaking her head sadly.

"It's harmless, or so Sabrina has convinced herself, but it's still unnerving to me."

"Well, that could be a good reason for making sure you spend time with her family as often as you can. You can be the balance to some of Arlene's goofiness and maybe keep her from making choices that wouldn't be good for her."

"I know," he agreed, standing as she rose from her seat. "Thanks for checking in with me."

Watching her walk out of the door, the realization that he hated what he had become washed over him. *I was a goddamn SEAL! Not some pussy who whines about his problems to others.* Taking a deep, cleansing breath, he began to tackle the mound of work on his desk.

Sabrina sighed heavily, staring at her phone for a moment after disconnecting with Jude. She ached for the man she had fallen in love with—the man she still loved. For over a year it had been agony as she watched him struggle with finding his way after his debilitating injury on his last mission. Rubbing her forehead, she thought back to the months of him pushing her away. *Stubborn man! Well, he found out that I'm just as stubborn.*

When things had been at their worst, she turned to

her cousin for advice. Chuckling to herself, she thought, *that's a sign of desperation...asking Bart Taggart for love advice! Mr. I'll Nail Anything with Boobs!* But as always, he came through for her. Explaining how the mind of a SEAL works, he encouraged her to not let Jude push her away. *"He doesn't get it now, Cuz, but he needs you. So you gotta be strong. You make him your mission and he'll come around."*

Going from his girlfriend and lover to being relegated to friend status hurt, but if it was the only way to stay close, then she took it.

Pulling her long hair back into a twist at the back of her head, she leaned over the fabric board she was working on. Her boss was thrilled that she brought a lot of business to the agency, but she knew Nonnie sent most of her friends over. Never one to ignore a gift, she could not help but wonder what it would be like to have her own business...away from Virginia Beach. *A place where I'm not known as Arlene's granddaughter, but just as Sabrina Taggart, Interior Designer.* Allowing her mind to wander, she smiled. *Sabrina Stedson also has a nice ring to it!*

Sobering, she heaved another sigh. *I'll never hear that unless Jude decides to take me off of the friend list.* She glanced out of the office window for a moment, battling the sting behind her eyes. Fighting the tears threatening, she closed her eyes. *Please God, help him.* The same prayer she had prayed for a year.

In the gym near his apartment, Jude worked his legs, continuing to strengthen them. The surgeries had given him a new knee, but also took away some of the damaged muscles in his calf. There was nothing he could do about the loss of muscle in his left leg, but he was determined to be as strong as possible.

The clink of the weight bars resounded through the almost empty room, but lent comfort as he moved his legs over and over. *At least I'm doing something*. He refused to attend a popular chain of gyms where he found most people were more concerned with what they were wearing than really working their bodies. The older building was used during the daytime by boxers and those training for MMA. Usually right after Jude got off of work, the gym was less crowded and he could work out without having to talk to anyone.

"You look fuckin' good with that," Cory Toller said, coming into the gym. A former SEAL also, Cory retired early to work in security. Their paths had crossed numerous times in the Navy, but lately Jude had seen him in the gym. He had also seen him occasionally at one of Sabrina's grandmother's parties since Cory's father-in-law was Senator Wilson, a friend of Arlene.

"Thanks, man," Jude replied, giving his legs a rest. "It's coming."

The two men settled in a companionable silence for a few minutes while each continued their workouts.

"How's the security business?" Jude asked.

"It's great. Keeps us busy and we're always looking for new people to bring on board," Cory replied. He let the weights fall back and pinned Jude with a stare.

"Look, man. I know you hate your job. Jared's always said there's a place for you with us if you're interested." Jared Rogers, a former SEAL, ran a security service.

Jude leaned his head against the worn, padded bench, heaving a sigh. Finally nodding, he said, "I appreciate it. Honestly, I really do. To think that you, Jared, and the others think I would be an asset means a lot."

"So what's holding you back? Surely it's not the paycheck or the pension."

"Nah. Truthfully?" Jude said, holding Cory's penetrating stare. "I always told myself that I'd get back to being a SEAL. If I worked harder, pushed myself just a little more, then I'd be able to keep my commission and my place with the team." Giving a rude snort, he continued, "I know to everyone else, it was a false hope, but it's what kept me going all those months when I forced myself to get out of the wheelchair, use the walker, then graduate to the crutches and then finally a cane."

"Nothing wrong with having that goal, bro," Cory replied. "If that's what it took to get you outta the hospital bed and on your feet, then there's nothing wrong with that."

Jude nodded slowly, the reality washing over him once more. "I know. And I accept the reality now. But gotta tell you that for months, my mind was SEALs or die." Heaving another sigh, he said, "Sabrina helped me realize that I have a lot to live for besides the team, but that was not an easy lesson to learn."

"You're one lucky fuck, you know? I can't tell you how many of our brothers came back home, injured or not, to girls that left them high and dry. Sabrina's a sweetheart."

"I know, believe me, I know," Jude responded, not willing to discuss the friends-only policy he had adopted with Sabrina. "I'll probably see you at some function her grandmother puts on. I'm sure your father-in-law will be invited."

Cory chuckled at the thought of Arlene Taggart. "Yeah, the Senator gets a hoot out of Mrs. Taggart. You never know what's gonna come outta her mouth. I mean she's really intelligent, but she's also kind of…"

"Flakey?" Jude interjected. "At least that's what Sabrina calls her."

The two men laughed as they continued their workout. After several minutes, Cory asked, "So, what now? You're in a job you hate and we've got work you could do. I know for a fact Jared and the others would love to have you."

Before he could answer, they were interrupted by a mutual friend walking into the gym. "Hell, yeah, Jared would love to have you," said Tom Byrd. Another medically retired SEAL, Tom had been stuck working security in a nuclear plant in Virginia until he went to work for Jared's company. "Best decision I ever made."

Nodding slowly once more, Jude replied, "I'll think about it. I really will, 'cause I need to get out of what I'm doing now."

With that, the three men continued their workout, the heavy conversation replaced with witty banter and camaraderie.

3

Jude moved toward the corner of the room, nearest the windows overlooking the perfectly manicured lawn. *God, I hate these parties.* It was not that he hated Arlene, but she always overdid things. His gaze moved around the packed room full of politicians, CEOs, and the local society high-brows. And while he could not hear their individual conversations, he knew what they were about. Stocks, bonds, investments. The newest up-and-coming politicians. The companies that were in trouble and which companies were merging. He closed his eyes for a moment wishing he could drown out the sounds just as easily.

Opening his eyes, he took a sip of the punch Arlene had provided. *Jesus, I just want a beer.* Sighing, his eyes found Sabrina, in another part of the room, trapped in a conversation with a matronly woman animatedly discussing...*who the fuck knows?*

Always beautiful, this time she was dressed in a mid-calf, light blue dress that swirled around her legs and ass when she walked. And the front certainly showed her assets off to perfection. He could not help but look around to see other men's eyes following her wherever she went.

Just as he started to rescue her, another woman approached and Sabrina appeared to be glad for the diversion. Turning back to stare out of the window again, he saw a large man walking toward him. A quick glance at the tall, blond, well-built man with an affable smile and Jude knew he was Sabrina's cousin, Bart.

Throwing his hand out for a shake, he acknowledged, "Bart, right? Good to see you again."

Bart's smile widened as he shook Jude's hand. "Good to see you, too. Sabrina talks a lot about you."

A tall, dark-haired man with a steely-eyed expression walked up and Bart made the introductions. "Jude, I'd like you to meet my boss, Jack Bryant."

After the initial handshakes and pleasantries, the three men stood awkwardly with the hubbub of the party swirling around them.

Bart looked at the patio just on the other side of the French doors and said, "Gentlemen, care to bust out of this joint? Love my grandmother, but her parties can really set my teeth on edge."

Jack and Jude chuckled and followed Bart out onto the patio, drinks in hand. Bart walked over to an outdoor refrigerator built into a stone bar at the edge of the patio. Grabbing three beers, he looked over with a smile. "Anyone want a beer?"

"God, yes," Jude answered, dumping his punch into a planter.

Away from the noise and boring conversations, the three men settled into the chairs and leaned back, instantly more at ease.

"Your grandmother's quite a lady," Jack commented, a grin on his face.

Bart snorted, "You don't have to be polite to me. She is a great lady, that's for sure, but it seems the older she gets, the battier she becomes." Bart looked over at Jude, saying, "I know you've been around her a lot more lately. Am I wrong?"

Jude deflected the question politely. "She's been very supportive of Sabrina. I know she's sent some of her friends to the design company Sabrina works for." He looked over to see the lifted eyebrow of Bart and then nodded his agreement. "Yeah, I have to say that in the last few months, she's been...um..." giving a shrug, "preoccupied."

"Preoccupied?" Jack asked, his curiosity piqued.

Jude noticed Bart leaned forward as well. Not knowing Bart well, he felt uncomfortable discussing the man's grandmother, but added, "She talks a lot about wanting to contact her late husband."

"Goddamnit!" Bart growled. "Who's she got working on it now?"

Jude shook his head. "I don't know any specifics. Sabrina has mentioned it several times." Wanting to turn the conversation to a more congenial topic, he looked over at Jack. The man was well-built, physically fit...*definitely former military, even with the longer hair and beard.* "Jack, were you prior service?"

Jack smiled and nodded. "Absolutely. Army. Special

Forces. I had the good fortune to be in a top-notch squad. I understand you were a SEAL?"

"Yeah, until my last mission when this leg got in the way of enemy fire," he grimaced, absently rubbing his left thigh. "New knee, but no more SEALs." *Jesus, I hate the way I sound so pathetic.*

"And now?" Jack asked.

Sucking in a deep breath before letting it out slowly, he pierced Jack with a steady stare. "I work at the Naval base here. Requisitions and logistics."

The men were quiet for a moment before Bart broke the silence. "And you hate your job, don't you?"

Jude looked over sharply. *Sabrina would never discuss my feelings with anyone. Am I so easy to read?*

Before he had a chance to speak, Bart jumped in again, "No offense, man. And Sabrina's said nothing. But it's just written all over you."

The noise of the party in the background filled the silence before he spoke. "Yeah. Honest to God…I hate it." He gave a rude snort and added, "But it's a job with a pension."

It did not escape his notice that Jack and Bart shared a glance before Jack spoke. "Sometimes it's hard to be in such a specialized military field and then try to find what the fuck you want to do when you leave. I have a buddy that was my Captain in the Special Forces. When he got out, he started a security company and has hired three other of our squad members along with others. They do security installations, provide security at functions, and have helped the police department in some of their investigations."

Jude, his attention piqued, nodded. "I've got some friends that are doing the same thing here. Former SEALs, most of them out and a few still in but helping on the side. They also take contracts that are...rather risky. And completely covert."

He felt the unasked question from both men and continued, "They've asked me to join them."

Bart, unable to imagine anyone wanting a desk job, cocked his head as he stared at Jude. "And you don't want to?"

Rubbing his hand over his face, Jude felt exposed. *How the hell did I end up talking about this to two men I don't even know?* Deciding he had nothing to lose, he continued. "Considering it. But to be honest, I've also considered moving somewhere else. This area..." he waved his hand around, "is full of good memories, but also a constant reminder of what I no longer can have."

He saw the expression on Bart's face and knew the other man was wondering about his cousin. Knowing Sabrina wanted more than friendship, her cousin had to be wondering about his abandoning her. In fact, he had to admit to himself the idea of moving away without her hurt almost as much the thought of her being with someone else.

Jack scratched his beard and said, "Told you what my former squad leader's business was, but I'm doing something similar. I started my own company. Saints Protection and Investigations. We do some security installs but mostly we investigate the crimes other agencies can't crack, don't have time for. Or just get bogged down in red-tape."

Jude, a spark of interest ignited, asked, "Is that what you do, Bart?"

Bart grinned, "Hell, yeah. I left the SEALs and did a year in Border Patrol. Got tired of the bureaucracy keeping us from doing our jobs and heard about Jack's business from a friend."

Shifting in his chair, Jack added, "My last Special Forces mission involved a multi-agency task force. I was doubtful it could work, but we clicked and I saw the benefit of working with a group of others with a variety of backgrounds and skills. So when I got out, I replicated that."

Just then the patio doors opened and out walked Sabrina and the beautiful woman she had been talking to. Before the women made their way over to them, Jack said, "Talk to Bart. If you really are interested, we can meet. You could be an asset to my team and it sounds like we may be what you're looking for."

Jude grinned, the feeling of hope pounding in his chest for the first time in a long time. "Will do."

"Hey guys," Sabrina greeted before turning to hug her cousin.

"Cuz," Bart said, returning the hug. "You're just as gorgeous as ever."

Jude introduced Jack to Sabrina and in turn was introduced to the other woman, Jack's wife, Bethany.

"I hate to break up your little party out here," Sabrina said, "but Nonnie wants to introduce us to someone."

Standing, Jude threw his arm around her shoulder. "Then lead on. We don't want to keep her waiting."

Jack and Bethany stayed on the patio as Bart, Sabrina, and Jude headed back through the French doors and over to Arlene. Her silver hair was perfectly coiffed and a pale yellow, silk afternoon dress spoke of elegance. As soon as her eyes landed on Sabrina and Jude, she smiled widely, moving toward them with her arms outstretched.

"My darlings, here you are! I want you to meet one of my dearest friends, Ruth Sewell." Arlene linked arms with a beautiful, elderly woman, smiling intently at them. She was smaller than Arlene but just as immaculately coiffed.

Sabrina moved in to shake her hand, but Ruth pulled her into a gentle hug. Sabrina moved back so Bart could greet his grandmother's friend.

"Oh, you are a big boy, aren't you?" Ruth said with a smile. "My husband was a big man too, God rest his soul."

Bart towered over the women, giving off his affable grin, as he shook her hand. She turned and Jude was introduced to her as well.

"Oh, you are the dear man here with Sabrina. I know Arlene is hoping for a wedding to plan, so you must get to that."

Sabrina blushed as Jude stumbled over his words, finally just saying, "Yes, ma'am," for lack of coming up with something better to say.

"You two lovebirds shouldn't waste time. You never know how long you might have with each other," Ruth continued. "Life just isn't the same without my dear, late husband. I sometimes don't know what to do without him."

Arlene moved back in to wrap her arm around Ruth's shoulders. "Well, that's why I'm introducing you to my new friend, Cecil Nastelli. If anyone can contact him, it is Cecil."

Sabrina quickly jerked her elbow into Bart's stomach to keep him from exploding. The others stood around in awkward silence as the two older women blissfully smiled at each other.

Arlene then turned to Sabrina, saying, "You should meet with him too. You will soon come into your trust and Cecil will help you to know what your grandfather would want you to do with the money."

Sabrina's grandfather arranged for a trust to come to her when she turned twenty-five years old, which was only a month away. She planned to open her own interior design business with the money. "Nonnie, I know what I'm going to do with the trust," she said.

"Oh, but my dear, I so wish you had your grandfather still with us. He was so wise with his money."

Glancing down at Sabrina, Jude could feel her apprehension. Pulling her a little closer, she looked up at him and gave a little appreciative smile. *It's the least I can do, baby.*

"You know I love you, but I'll be damned if I stand around and let some phony take you for a ride and drag Sabrina along with you!"

The tone of Bart's voice was unmistakable in its anger. Jack and Bethany had left when the party disbanded, and now just the members of the family were ensconced in the comfortable family room of Arlene's home.

"Bartholomew!" Arlene spoke sharply. "I will not allow you to talk about Mr. Nastelli like that. He's a very good friend."

"Friend?" he sputtered.

"Yes, a friend. He comforts me."

Sabrina stepped in between her cousin and her grandmother, mediating as usual. "Nonnie, it's okay. Bart didn't mean to imply that Mr. Nastelli isn't a friend. We just want to make sure you're all right."

"Humph. Of course, I'm all right," Arlene defended herself.

Bart sat heavily on the sofa, where Jude had already taken a seat. The two men passed a look of sympathy between them, as Bart ran his hand through his hair causing the ends to stick up.

Sabrina continued, "We're just concerned about what he's telling you about granddad."

"I can appreciate that, my dear," Arlene said, patting Sabrina's arm. "So far, he's only made contact with John twice. And both times, he said he needs a little more time to understand what John is directing him to do. Cecil's so wise in these matters."

Sabrina shot a look of confusion at her grandmother first and then over to Jude, before asking, "Wise in what matters?"

"Well, he thinks John is trying to communicate with me."

At that, Sabrina's mouth open and closed several times but no words came out. Bart stood quickly again, this time walking over to kneel in front of his grandmother's seat.

"Nonnie, you know granddad has been…gone now for five years?" he questioned her gently.

"Yes, of course, I know. I'm not daffy!"

"Then how can he be telling you what you should do?" Sabrina finally found her voice.

"Mr. Nastelli can call John's spirit to be here. You just have to believe in him, my dear. He reveals everything," Arlene explained patiently as though talking to recalcitrant children.

"Well, as long as it makes you happy…" Sabrina's voice trailed off as Bart's angry expression silenced her.

After a few more conciliatory assurances from Arlene, the others left Arlene's mansion and headed to the restaurant where they were going to meet Jack and Bethany for drinks.

Walking into the lively restaurant, they quickly saw their friends in a large booth near the back. Bart caught the eye of the waitress, winking at her as he pointed toward the table. She hurried over to take their beer orders, trying without success to grab Bart's continued attention.

Once settled in the booth, Bart rounded on his cousin. "What the hell was that, Sabrina? You just allow Nonnie to feed into that shit."

"Not cool, bro," Jude interjected rapidly. "Don't take

your frustrations about your grandmother out on Sabrina."

Sabrina smiled up at him, leaning in a little more as she rested her back into his side.

"What's going on?" Bethany asked, unable to keep the curiosity to herself.

Before Bart could explode his explanation, Sabrina hurried to say, "My grandmother has been looking for mediums for the past several years that will allow her to talk to my grandfather, ever since he died."

"Voices from the great beyond," Bart whispered, his voice sounding like a B-horror movie narrator. The searing look from Sabrina shut him up, but not before he managed another eye roll toward her.

Bethany said, "But if he's not causing any harm and if the diversion makes your grandmother happy—"

"Exactly!" Sabrina agreed, turning to her cousin. "It hurts no one for her to find this little way to make her happy."

Bart lifted an eyebrow and said, "Yeah, but what about what he may be telling her?"

At that, Sabrina deflated a little, sinking more into Jude's warm embrace. She twisted around to look into his face. "Am I doing the wrong thing, Jude? I trust your opinion."

"Sabrina, I'm coming into this kind of blind," Jude admitted. "I honestly don't get a good vibe about him, but I've got nothing to base that on other than my gut."

Jack, who had been silent up to this point, commented, "It may seem innocent, but if this guy is some kind of a con-artist..."

"That's what I think," Bart agreed, lifting his hand for the waitress to send him another beer, ignoring the lustful look she bestowed on him.

Jude, now on alert, said, "I'll be damned if I'll let someone take advantage of Sabrina or Arlene. Is there something we can do?"

Jack nodded, his dark eyes ever alert, adding, "I'll have one of my men do a quick background check."

"Luke?" Bart asked, knowing Luke was Jack's best man for computer searches. Receiving a nod, Bart added, "He finds anything, I'll be paying a visit to the good Mr. Nastelli."

"And I'll be going with you," Jude said, feeling the spark that used to accompany the beginning of a mission. He allowed his mind to begin calculating possibilities, something that had been dormant since the accident. After a moment, he added, "No. We need to go slow. If it does turn out to be something then we shouldn't go in with guns blazing."

Bart looked at him incredulously, but before he could say anything, Jack was already nodding his agreement.

Jude sat up straighter, saying, "Look, if this guy is actually doing harm, I want to know exactly what he's doing and who all he's doing it to. And there's no way a con artist is going to talk to anyone who looks like us."

Bethany laughed. "Oh yeah. You guys definitely look intimidating and there's no way you can pull off trying to look innocent!"

At that, Sabrina smiled. "I hadn't thought about it,

but that's right. Just one look at you all and the image screams *I'm gonna kick your ass!*"

The group chuckled just as the waitress, once more trying to catch Bart's eye, brought his beer. Ignoring her again, she stomped away, eliciting more laughs from the group.

He glared, saying, "What? Ya'll act like I never say 'no'."

With a raised eyebrow, Sabrina replied, "That's because you never do!"

His natural grin returned as he agreed. "Yeah, well, I may have to make it up to her on the way out."

Bringing the conversation back to Arlene, Jack interjected, "You can bet your grandmother isn't the only one taken in with this guy." Looking at Bart and then swinging his appraising eye toward Jude, he continued, "I'll let you know what Luke finds and then you can plan how you want to handle it."

Sabrina watched the play of emotions cross Jude's face and smiled. She had not seen this level of interest in him in a long time. *Jude, if you would just open your eyes to all the possibilities. Careers out there that you would love to do. And me...right in front of you, wanting nothing more than to love you.*

"Revealed? Fuckin' *revealed?*" Bart's voice exploded over the phone.

"That's what he said to Arlene. That your grandfather would speak to him and then, in turn, he will let

33

your grandmother and Sabrina know how to invest their money."

A week had passed before Jude and Sabrina met with her grandmother once again, trying to gain more information on what Nastelli's angle, and now they knew. Cecil was aiming to coerce Arlene with her investments.

"I gotta get back to Virginia Beach to talk to Nonnie, but I'm in the middle of an investigation that has me tied up. Let me talk to Jack and see if I can get some time off."

"Listen, Bart," Jude said. "Right now, if you come here blowing up at Arlene and Cecil, then you're just going to upset her and maybe make him go into hiding until he moves on to his next mark. Why don't you let me work the problem from here?"

Silence met his suggestion, but Jude knew Bart was smart and methodical. Finally, he heard a sigh on the other end of the phone.

"You're right. I know you're right. I just want to pound this guy into the ground and sitting back goes against my nature."

"Think of your SEAL training, just like you told me. We plan the mission. We execute the mission. That's the best way to not only get him away from your family, but take him down for good." For the first time, Jude was using his SEAL experience in the civilian world and it was not causing the twinge of familiar pain. *Instead, it feels fuckin' good!*

"Got one more thing to talk over with you," Jude said. "It has to do with Sabrina."

"Thank fuck," Bart responded quickly. "It's about time you got your head outta your ass and went after her."

"Huh?"

"Isn't that what you were going to say? That the two of you stopped dancing around each other and finally decided to become a couple?"

"No," Jude said regretfully.

Before he could say anything else, Bart jumped in. "Why the fuck not? She's been in love with you for over a year. What's wrong with her that you don't want her too?"

"You don't know what you're talking about," Jude bit out.

"No?" Bart shot back. "I know you're in love with her and SEALs don't pussy out, man."

"I'm not a SEAL anymore, remember?"

"Fuck that. I got out, but once a SEAL, always a SEAL."

Sucking in a deep breath, Jude said, "I do love her." Letting out the breath slowly, he continued, "But until I can be the man I think she deserves, then we're just friends."

Silence reached across the airwaves for a moment before Bart said, "I get that. I do and I even respect that. But what you gotta realize is that she loves you, not any label you put on yourself. And even though I think she'll wait...you better make a move before someone else does."

A white-hot bolt of jealousy ripped through Jude at the thought of Sabrina in another man's arms, but he pushed the image down, focusing on the matter at hand. "Any chance you could get Jack to let me use Luke for some more computer digging? I've got a bad feeling about this Nastelli and Sabrina. Arlene's mentioned Sabrina's trust and I'm afraid she's going to try to get this guy working on Sabrina as well."

"Absolutely. In fact, Jack's already said he wants in on this," Bart answered immediately.

"Perfect." The idea of working with Jack's team on this investigation lifted Jude's spirits. The desire to protect Sabrina and her family was strong and with Saints Protection & Investigation at his back, he just might be able to do it.

"Can you be ready for a conference call later this afternoon? I'll get things set up on our end and then call you in about two hours."

Tossing his cell phone onto the table, Jude could feel the energy begin a slow burn through his veins. Being active, planning, doing something...*anything*...besides sitting at his desk shoving papers from one side to the other, felt good.

He glanced around at his first-floor apartment, the one he rented when he was in a wheelchair. *No view. Nothing special.* And now, staring at the handicapped-accessible kitchen off to the side, he began to long for a different place to live. *But the next place I live, I want Sabrina there with me.*

Then his mind slid to Bart's warning about Sabrina. *She loves you. She'll probably wait for you. Don't miss your chance.* Heaving a heavy sigh, he wondered what to do. *Tell her I love her now or wait until I can be a better man?*

4

Cecil sat at the only table in his condo, tapping furiously on his laptop. He pulled up searches on Arlene and John Taggart, as well as Ruth Sewell and a few others. Making sure his printer had enough paper, he began printing out articles he found. The wealthy always managed to get in the newspaper society pages, as well as the business sections. He smiled to himself as he found fodder for his deception. Photographs. Articles. Even the obituaries provided what he needed. *This will be so simple. Hell, forget taking candy from a baby, nothing's as easy as fooling a rich, old woman!*

Cecil's training had started early. *"It's in your blood, boy,"* dad used to say. *"It's all about emotion. Tap into someone's emotion and you can get rich!"*

He remembered as a small boy, his father would put them in the family car, park on the side of the road and get passing motorists to give him money to buy gasoline after telling them their car ran out of gas.

He thought back to his mother, the perfect organization's fundraiser. Except she never worked for any organization...other than his father's will. She would go door to door, dressed immaculately, with her literature for cancer funds, children's homes, even the local police annual fund drive. Ringing doorbells, she presented the perfect picture for trusting individuals, many who would give her an inordinate amount of cash.

His parents had probably tried—and succeeded—at hundreds of cons. Or at least, they stayed one step ahead of the law. Land schemes, selling counterfeit watches, telemarketing frauds, even selling false cemetery plots.

"Son, the rich will never miss the money we take. Hell, they think they're doing a good deed, so they don't care. And you think anyone rich got that way legally? They're just bigger crooks, that's all."

His parents had died years earlier, but Cecil smiled as he continued their legacy. *There's no reason I can't have the good life too!*

The smile left his face as he checked his email, seeing another reminder about the money he owed. Running his hand through his hair, he growled. The crippling interest on the money he borrowed threatened his livelihood. Glancing around at his bare, expensive living quarters, he grimaced once more. The location was purely for show, in case someone checked on where he lived, but the cost was taking most of what he earned on the last gig after making a payment on what he owed.

Fuck! I should have never borrowed the money, he chastised himself. His last mark had spooked at the last minute and Cecil had to leave North Carolina quickly.

Arriving in the Virginia Beach area, he needed the ready cash to start over. *I've got this, I know I do. No way is old lady Taggart going to back out of finding what her precious John wants her to do.* He knew this latest score had to hit. And hit huge in order for him to pay back the loan. Another piece of his dad's advice was coming back to bite him in the ass. *"Don't try to scam another scammer. You could lose big."*

Sucking in a huge breath, he once again turned his attention to the articles, determined to learn everything he could about his next marks.

Jude sat outside of the tall, glass and brick condo building in downtown Virginia Beach, waiting to catch a glimpse of Cecil. *How the hell does he afford to live in a place this fancy?* It was not easy to locate his home and Jude could not have done it on his own. Since Luke had determined Cecil Nastelli did not actually exist with a birth certificate, he was able to locate his residence based on the cell phone information he managed to finagle from Arlene on the pretext that he needed to talk to Cecil. Armed with that info, Jude had been sitting in his car for three hours waiting to follow the man as soon as he showed himself. Even the tedious exercise still gave him more of a burst of enthusiasm than his job. *I need to think about quitting if I'm serious about moving and possibly working for Jack.* Taking another sip of his now-cold coffee, *and I've got to talk to Sabrina. I don't want to go without her. But will she want to go?*

Before he could continue that train of thought, he saw Cecil walk out the front doors and move briskly down the street. *He's walking with a purpose and not just a stroll.* He watched as Cecil lifted his hand to hail a taxi and Jude was primed to pull out behind them. Just then a flash of color caught his eye. There was a woman wearing a red scarf, large sunglasses, and a coat hustling behind Cecil, waving to hail another cab. *What the fuck? I'd know that woman anywhere and in any disguise.*

Pulling his car right up beside her, he rolled down his window and barked, "Get in!"

The woman jumped backward in surprise, before peering inside the vehicle. "Jude? Wha—"

"Get the fuck in, Sabrina," he said, his voice barely above a growl. "Now!"

She hustled over and hopped into the passenger side, buckling quickly as he pulled out into traffic, the taxicab still in front of him.

She opened her mouth to speak, but he got there first. "You want to tell me what the hell you're doing?"

"I'm trying to help Nonnie," she said, righteous indignation punctuating each word. "Why are you here?"

"I told you that I would work with Bart to see what we could come up with. You should have waited for me."

She twisted in her seat, her glare boring a hole through him. "You never told me you were actively doing anything like this. How was I supposed to know what you were doing?"

"I purposefully left you out thinking it would protect you," he argued back.

"Jude, I don't need protecting. I can take care of myself, but would have gladly worked with you if you had told me."

"Well, you weren't exactly forthcoming when you said you were busy this afternoon," he accused, referring to their earlier phone conversation.

"I didn't lie—I am busy!" she said, crossing her arms over her chest.

"Yeah, busy being seen!" He glanced over at her outfit, trying to stay irritated when a chuckle threatened to erupt. "Babe, seriously? A bright red scarf and sunglasses on a cloudy day. You practically scream, *Here I am!*"

Sabrina continued to glare but soon realized her pouting was counter-productive. Pulling the scarf off her head with a jerk, she said, "I guess my outfit does look silly. I just didn't want him to recognize me."

Heaving a sigh, he said, "You shouldn't be in this at all, Sabrina. I don't like this guy. I don't trust this guy. And I certainly don't want you anywhere near this guy." He gave her a pointed stare. "By the way, how did you know where he lived? I had to get Bart and Luke on it."

"I lucked out. He was just leaving Nonnie's yesterday and he didn't see me so I followed him."

"Impressive," Jude pronounced, a smile on his lips.

"We make a good team, don't you think?" she said, hope in her voice.

He turned to look at her beautiful face staring at his. *Bart says she loves me, but how long will she wait if I keep saying we can only be friends? I know I love her, so maybe it's time to do something about it...before it's too late!*

Before he could speak, she said, "Look!"

Jude saw Cecil's taxi pull up to a gated community on the outskirts of Virginia Beach and gain access to the area. Stuck on the outside, Jude cursed. Turning back to Sabrina, he said, "You got any ideas on who he might be visiting?"

"No," she said, shaking her head in frustration. Looking over, she said, "How about we put our heads together and see what we can figure out."

Grinning, he nodded. "Putting our heads together might be just the thing we need to do."

Pizza boxes and empty beer bottles covered the old, scarred coffee table as Jude and Sabrina piled up on the comfortable sofa in Jude's apartment a few hours later.

Jude worked on his laptop, banging away on the keyboard while occasionally emitting groans of frustration. "This guy is totally in the wind. There's no virtual footprint that I can find." Finally setting his computer to the side, he said, "I'm gonna have to leave that to Luke and focus on what I can do here."

Looking over at him, she said, "You know more about what Bart does than I do."

Shrugging, he said, "His job interested me when we

met and especially after talking to his boss, Jack. It's something that I would consider."

"Well, I think you should definitely think of doing investigations instead of the job you have now, which you hate." Leaning over, she placed her hand on his muscular arm, "I just want to see you happy."

Turning, he stared into her wide, blue eyes. Her face was so close and his gaze dropped to her luscious mouth, pink wet lips slightly open.

"What would you say if I told you that I was thinking about working in security?" he said softly, watching carefully for her reaction.

"I know how miserable you are in your current job, so I'd be thrilled for you," she replied.

Come on, man up, he told himself, watching the sadness slip into her eyes. "Sabrina?" he said softly, reaching out his hand, rubbing his knuckles over her silky cheek. He watched as she lifted her eyes back to his and recognized a flash of hope in them.

"I've...I...I wanted us to just be friends because... well, quite frankly, I wasn't very happy with myself. When being a SEAL was taken from me, I felt...incomplete, and I wasn't in a good place to be with someone romantically if I wasn't a whole man."

Her eyebrows drew together in question as she cocked her head to the side. "I know that, Jude. I tried to fight your stubborn pride for a long time before finally giving in to just being friends."

Once more, the silence filled the space between them, this time slightly less heavy.

She licked her lips nervously, asking, "Is...um...

something different now?" Her gaze drifted to his laptop and the notes she had been taking. "Does this make a difference?" she asked, pointing to evidence of their work.

He leaned back on the sofa and heaved a sigh. "Yeah, I guess it does. I know this may sound stupid, but for the first time in a long time, I feel excited to be working on something. I started out wanting to do this for you. I want to make sure you're not taken advantage of, but then this is snowballing into proving I can plan and execute a mission that has nothing to do with the SEALs."

She quietly watched the play of emotions cross his handsome face but smiled as she saw the slow grin. She had wanted him to find a place of peace for a year and watching it happen was like watching the sunrise on what you just knew was going to be a great day.

He tilted his head back, sighing, as he gazed up to the ceiling. "I had one of those days where the tedious duties of my job are so different from what I was doing as a SEAL, that I felt as though I would choke on the boredom. Lucy noticed and I felt like a pussy complaining to her." He brought his head back down and met her gaze. "Then at the gym, I ran into Cory , wanting me to go work for Jared. It's their security business."

"Is that what you want to do?" she asked, twisting her body so she was looking into his face. "Because if it is, you know that would be fine with me."

"I don't know. I don't know what jobs they would have for me." He sighed again, his thoughts churning. "I guess I could consider it. There is something else, but I don't know how you feel about it."

Now he had her rapt attention. "Okay…" she prompted.

His eyes met hers as he leaned forward once more. "There's one more thing I have to do before I can be ready to make this change in my life. And that's to make sure that you're with me." He watched the confused expression morph into curiosity. She cocked her head to the side once more, the silent question reaching across the space.

"I tried so hard to push you away when I was injured, but you just wouldn't leave me alone. But I knew that I couldn't give you what you needed. Not then. Not when I still had so much to prove to myself. Learn about myself. Figure out on my own."

A tear dropped to her cheek and he wiped it gently with the rough pad of his thumb. Plunging on, he said, "I want to take this next step in my life. If I decide to do the investigating, I'd have to quit the job as a civilian with the Navy to try something new."

Sabrina stayed silent, another tear following the path of the first one, once more gently wiped away.

"But I don't want to make that kind of life-changing decision without you, my best friend," he added.

Swallowing loudly, her head dropped as she fought the emotions ripping through her. *This is what I wanted,* she told herself. *For him to be happy.* She tried to calm her shaking voice as she assured, "Jude, I've always only wanted what was best for you. And if this change is right, then you have to take it."

Letting out the breath he had been holding, a smile spread across his face. "Oh, babe, that's just what I wanted to hear."

Her lips parted but no words followed, surprise on her face. As he caressed her cheek once more, she leaned her face into his large, warm hand. *Please say what I think you're saying, Jude,* she silently begged.

"I've loved you since the first day I met you," he confessed. "I wanted you, claimed you, and planned on making you my wife."

Another tear formed in the corner of her eye and stayed there, hanging on her lashes. He watched it, fascinated, as he continued.

"Maybe I've waited too long..." his voice drifted off, anguish in his eyes.

Sabrina bolted from her seat, throwing her arms around his neck, crying and saying, "No, no. Never too long. I love you, too."

5

As the rush of emotions crashed over the two, Jude pulled Sabrina's face toward his, latching onto her mouth in a kiss. Plunging his tongue between her rosy lips, he re-discovered all of the treasures he had found when he first kissed her. Once more within her warm mouth, he wondered how he ever held her at arm's length for so long.

Angling her head for better access, he continued to plunder, swallowing her moans as his own sounds were ringing in his ears.

Her fingers initially grasped the front his t-shirt before shifting to the bottom, pulling the soft material upward, a grunt of frustration emitting when she could not get it off.

He leaned back just long enough for her to pull it the rest of the way over his head before tossing the shirt onto the floor. Reciprocating, she allowed him to pull her sweater off as well, letting it land on the coffee table.

A silver medallion dangled from around his neck, catching her attention as she did not recognize it. *He never used to wear a saint's medallion.*

He caught her curious gaze as he fingered the object. Answering her unasked question, he said, "It's a St. Jude medallion. After I'd been injured, a priest came to visit me in the hospital. I was pretty pissed he was even implying that I might not be able to return to my team. As he left, he said it was interesting that St. Jude was the patron saint of the impossible...of lost causes. When I finally realized that I wasn't going to be able to stay a SEAL, I was so angry. I saw this in a shop a few months ago and on a whim I bought it."

His eyes went from the medallion to her face and saw her soft gaze on his.

"I'm so sorry, Jude. For everything."

"Yeah, well, maybe I am a lost cause," he muttered.

"No, no. You're not a lost cause," she refuted. "But sometimes hanging on to the past and not looking forward is the lost cause." She lifted her hand and fingered the medallion. "Maybe the Saint works. After all, you thought we were a lost cause."

Listening to her words flow over him, he could not keep the smile from his lips. "You may be right. I thought we were impossible...and now? You're here in my arms once more."

Locking lips again, he moved his mouth over hers, remembering the feel of her soft flesh as it melded with his. She sucked on his tongue and he felt his cock swell painfully in his jeans. Kissing down her jawline, he dipped to the indentation where her shoulders met her neck, sucking on her pulse point. She arched her back, her breasts pushing against his chest, feeling the material of the bra abrade her sensitive nipples.

Unclasping the offending material, he slid it off her body, freeing the rosy-tipped, full breasts that he so missed. They bounced as the bra flew across the room, landing near the lamp on the end table. Lifting his hands to her breasts, he felt their weight as his thumbs rubbed and then tweaked her nipples, once more catching her groan in his mouth.

"I want..." she said between kisses.

"Yeah," was his reply, as he stood with her in his arms, walking down the hall leading to his bedroom. He swung to the left to keep her head from hitting the wall but banged her feet on the doorframe. Her grunt was interrupted by his kiss, as he staggered into the room, tossing her onto the bed.

"Smooth move, sailor-boy," she giggled.

Watching her breasts bounce, he fell on top of her, careful to hold his weight up on his forearms. "Keep watching, baby-doll. I've got all kinds of smooth moves."

Latching onto a rosy nipple, he sucked, nipped, licked, circling his tongue around the distended flesh before moving to the other one. Writhing on the bed, she pushed her hips up, coming into contact with the evidence of his arousal.

Her hand drifted down between them, palming the bulge in his pants. After a moment, he reached down to capture her wrist, pulling it upward over her head. She started to protest, but he said, "Can't baby. I'll be finished before we get started. It's been so fuckin' long."

Her sex-induced fog lifted momentarily, allowing her to focus on his words. *Been so fuckin' long? Has he—*

"I can hear the question in your head," he said, lifting his head from her breasts. "And the answer is no. I haven't been with anyone else since you."

"Really?" she asked, her blue eyes wide as they focused on his face framed by the wavy hair she so loved.

"Babe, I've been in love with you this whole time. Why would I be with someone else when you were the only one I wanted?"

"I didn't know," she confessed. "I thought maybe just being friends meant that you had...well, gotten your needs...um...met some other way."

He watched as a blush started from the tops of her breasts rising to her face. Remembering the stupid show he put on the night he left the bar with a pretend hookup just to try to push Sabrina away, he hung his head. Pulling himself up her body, he kissed the blush trail until he landed on her lips once more. "I was an ass that night and I'm so sorry for hurting you. I left that woman in the parking lot."

He watched Sabrina's adorable, confused expression and continued, "I never intended for anything to happen with her. You've been it for me. The reason I worked so hard to recuperate. The reason I was determined to find something that I loved doing, so that I could once again feel like the kind of man you deserved."

"You never had to prove anything to me," she

protested, then quickly added, "But I know you felt as though you did."

Her acknowledgment of his feelings poured over him, the warmth moving through his veins. Before he could say anything else, she whispered against his lips, "Please, make love to me."

Needing no further encouragement, he rose from the bed and slipped her pants down her legs, snagging her silky, pink panties as he went. Her naked body lay exposed to his perusal and his breath caught in his throat as she presented herself to him. *More beautiful than I remembered.*

Her gaze dipped to his jeans, the bulge pressing against his zipper. "I think one of us is overdressed."

With a wink, he shucked his jeans and boxers after toeing off his boots. Climbing back over her body, he began a slow exploration once more, starting with her legs. Running his fingers and lips along the delicious curves, he circled his tongue around her belly-button, the tickling motion causing her to squirm and giggle.

Moving his lips back to her breasts, his fingers trailed along her moist slit, slipping into the prize. Her inner walls were slick and tight and he quickly found the spot and the rhythm to cause her giggles to turn into moans.

Grasping the sheets in her fists, Sabrina leaned her head up, mesmerized while watching her nipples disappear in his mouth and feeling the jolts of electricity zinging from deep inside where his fingers worked their magic. A tear slid to the sheet, the fear that she would never share this with him again finally letting go.

"Baby?" he asked, stilling his fingers. "What's wrong?"

"Oh, nothing," she croaked. "I'm just happy."

"Yeah?" he asked, a sly smile on his face. "Well, if you're happy with just this, wait until you see what all I have in store for you."

Biting her bottom lip, she then moaned as his fingers continued their exploration. Within a few minutes, she knew her orgasm was close and slid her hand down to her clit. His other hand quickly replaced hers and with a few tweaks, she threw her head back as her first non-self-induced orgasm in over year ripped through her.

Riding out the waves of ecstasy, she slowly floated back to consciousness and noticed his sexy grin beaming down on her.

"Hmph," she grunted. "You look pretty satisfied with yourself."

"Me? I'd say from that scream, you were the one who was satisfied."

Laughing, she admitted, "Okay, you got me. That was amazing!"

"Amazing? Now that's what I like to hear," he boasted.

"You were in doubt?"

He peered down at her, lightly brushing her thick, auburn hair from her face so he could see every nuance of her expression. "I was never in doubt about what you could do to me. I was just in doubt about me."

Lifting her hand, she cupped his jaw. I love you, Jude Stedson."

Moving his body over hers with his cock at her

entrance, he gently kissed her lips and said, "And I love you, too." With that, she opened her legs wide and he slipped inside. As soon as he entered her warm sex, he stilled, eyes wide.

"Oh, God, I forgot a condom," he confessed.

"It's okay. I'm still on the pill," she said. "And if neither of us has been with anyone since each other, then we're good."

"Thank fuck!" he exclaimed, pulling out before plunging in once more. Quickly finding his rhythm, he moved slowly at first and then with her urging, began pistoning faster. "Baby, I'm not gonna be able to last long, no matter how much self-control I have. Are you close?"

"Yes, yes," she cried, moving her hand to her clit, tapping the swollen nub. She could feel her core tighten and as he lowered his mouth to tug on her nipple, the combination sent her flying. Screaming once more, she saw his head rear back and offer her a delectable view of his tight neck muscles as he powered through his own release. Thrusting until the last drop wrung out of him, he fell to the side, pulling her with him.

Several minutes passed, no word spoken as each slowly came down from their euphoric high. As their breathing evened out and their bodies began to cool, he snagged the blanket to cover them. They continued to lay for several more minutes, no words necessary as his arms wrapped around her and her head rested on his chest.

"Wow," she whispered. Her head jiggled as his chuckle rumbled through his chest.

"You can say that again."

"So...um...what exactly...I mean...where do we go from here?" she asked, unable to hide all of the doubt in her voice.

He immediately rolled over so that he was on his side as he looked down at her, his hand cupping her cheek. "I'm so sorry, baby, that I couldn't be what you needed since my injury. I just...lost myself."

"I know," she smiled, "but knew you would find yourself again. That's why I waited. Well, that and if the only part of you I could have was your friendship, then I would take whatever I could have."

"Baby, I want it all. You, me, a life together, and no more pushing away. I promise you that."

Her smile was her reply.

He hesitated, watching her face closely once more. "And if I decide that I need to have a career change?"

Smiling brightly, she said, "I'll be right with you. I'll support you in any way that I can."

He kissed her gently once more, this time the promise of many more kisses were felt on her lips.

The next morning as the sun slipped in through the blinds, Sabrina looked around Jude's bedroom, seeing the sparse décor. A single dresser was against the wall next to the wide-door closet and the bed. That was it. She knew he moved into this apartment when he was wheelchair bound but wondered at the lack of personality. She looked over at him as he slept. *Almost like him. Not knowing who he was.*

She rolled to her side with her head in her hands, watching him. A smile moved across her face as she took in the day-old stubble on his strong jaw. His sandy blond hair curled on the ends and she realized that she had no idea what it would look like when his hair grew out from the military regulation haircut he had always sported. And seeing the curls, she could not wait to run her fingers through the thickness. Before she could give in to the desire, his eyes opened, pinning her to the spot.

"Hey," he greeted with a sleepy growl, rolling toward her as his lips instinctively found hers.

After he moved back to see her face more clearly, he noticed the crease in her brow. "Hmmm, I know what that means. Your wheels are turning," he commented.

"I just thought since you want to consider doing investigations as a possible job, then maybe you should get Bart or his boss, Jack, involved in how we should proceed with this mess."

"We? Babe, there is no *we* in this."

"You know what Jack said. If Nastelli gets a hint you're checking him out then he'll leave town. I thought you all wanted to stop him from doing this to other vulnerable women."

"I know, but maybe I can convince him that I want to use his services."

Shaking her head, she said, "Look, Jude. I've been thinking about this. Nonnie has already talked to Mr. Nastelli about me and my trust. Maybe I could meet with him, convince him that I'm interested and see what that gets us."

"Hell, no!" he shouted, sitting up in the bed. "I don't want you near this guy!"

Arguing for several more minutes, Sabrina flopped back down on the bed in frustration. "Fine. Then talk to Jack. See what he thinks."

Reluctantly agreeing, he called Bart later that morning, after she went to work, and within a few minutes had Jack on the line. Much to his chagrin, Jack agreed with Sabrina.

"Look, Jude. Do your research first when planning a mission. No con artist that is as good as this guy is, will ever talk to you. He's smart and his self-preservation is at an all-time high. Tell you what, we'll do a phone conference with you and my group when you get a little more information to see what the next course of action should be."

Jude agreed, then called Sabrina back. "I'm going to work with Jack's group on this and if, and only if, they think we have no other choice, then you can help."

After getting her agreement to not act independently, he disconnected the call and leaned back on the sofa, running his hands through his hair once more. *Jesus, Bart makes this sound so easy. Hell, so do Cory and Rick. If this is going to be my new career and keep Sabrina in my life...I've got to figure out how to make this work.*

6

"Arlene?" Jude spoke on his cell phone. "Sabrina and I were wondering if you knew anyone in Clairmont Estates? I heard of some break-ins in that neighborhood and we're trying to think of some friends of yours that might live there?"

Sabrina rolled her eyes as his deception but had to admit he was convincing. Clairmont Estates was the gated community Cecil had disappeared into and they wondered if he had other marks he was targeting.

"Um-hm…um-hm…" he murmured as he quickly wrote on a pad of paper. "Okay, thank you," he said. "No, no, nothing major. Sabrina and I were just trying to think of some people we knew there."

Getting off the phone, he looked shocked. "I swear, your grandmother knows everyone around."

"So, any good possibilities?"

"I wrote down about five names, but only one really hit home. Ruth Sewell. The woman she introduced us to at her party. Turns out she's Governor Sewell's widowed mother."

"Oh, my God! I never made the connection. What should we do?"

"Let's have Arlene invite her for tea, we'll casually find out if she has introduced Ruth to Cecil and then I'm letting Jack know. He has previously taken on contracted work for the governor before and I want his input."

"This is getting more complex than just a man trying to cozy up to Nonnie," she said, worry furrowing her brow.

"I got this, babe," he assured, leaning over to steal a kiss. "I'm working the problem."

"Jude?" Bart confirmed as he settled back into his chair, the other Saints on the screen.

"Good to see you all," Jude said, slightly nervous at meeting Jack's crew. He could see four men in the camera's view and knew several more were off camera.

Bart made the introductions and then turned it over to Jude.

"Thank you for agreeing to confer with me on this. I know Bart has informed you of what we're looking into. I'm sure Cecil Nastelli is a con artist. It looks like he probably searches out wealthy widows and tries to fleece them out of money by pretending to be a medium who can communicate with their deceased husbands to find out what they would want the widows to do with their money or how to invest. But," he added hesitantly, "I have no proof yet as to exactly what he's doing."

"Sounds like you're on the right track," Jack commented, looking up from the notes he was typing. "Bart said there were others?"

"Yes. I've now gotten confirmation that he's been meeting with Governor Sewell's widowed mother. She lives in Virginia Beach and we found out she's one of the women he's been working with."

"Goddamn," Jack swore. "I've met Ruth Sewell before. Sweet lady. Very smart as well, but I've heard that in the last several years, her mind is a little less sharp. That'd make her a perfect target for someone like Nastelli."

Jude cleared his throat before plunging forward. "Jack, I was hoping I could continue to investigate what's going on here, but perhaps with your connection to the governor, would also be able to call upon your business' assistance when needed. As long as I wasn't interrupting any of your current investigations, of course," he added quickly.

Jack looked up sharply and then over to Bart, before looking back. "Jude, you don't have to worry about our involvement. This is dealing with Bart's family and we take care of our own. So you have our full support and resources." Grinning, he added, "Can I be hopeful that you're considering coming to work for me?"

Smiling back, Jude said, "Yes, sir. I'm very much considering it. I want to complete this investigation and then will want to meet with you to discuss the possibility. I would need to turn in my resignation with the Navy as long as you and I are in agreement."

"Coming alone?" Bart asked.

"Nope," he answered quickly. "At least I hope not." Sheepishly looking into the camera at Bart, he added, "Sabrina and I are together now—"

"It's 'bout fuckin' time," Bart quipped.

"But I haven't mentioned the possibility of moving yet. It felt...too soon," he warned.

The Saints and Jude continued planning for several more minutes. Jack assured him that he would report to the governor and that Jude was sanctioned to proceed.

Jack said, "What about Sabrina? Does she still want to try to meet with Nastelli?"

Sighing heavily, Jude nodded. "Yeah, she's dying to do something to protect her grandmother. I just don't want her in danger."

"Absolutely agreed," Jack said. "Why don't we set up another conference with her included?"

With the next virtual meeting scheduled, Jude leaned back. A smile on his face, he felt like thumping his chest. *Got the job offer I want. Got the girl. Now just gotta get the asshole trying to steal from her and her family.*

"Good to see you again, Sabrina," Jack said easily into the camera.

Nervously fidgeting with her fingers, Sabrina gave a tentative smile back. "Nice to see you also."

Jack had his camera pan around to show the other

members of his team that were present, all with smiles for her, with the exception of a scowling Bart.

When the camera landed on her cousin, he admitted, "I don't like this, but Jack's right about what we need to do to catch this slick-shit."

The camera swung over to a stylish, debonair man introduced as Monty. With a nod, he began, "I've got undercover experience so Jack wants me to give you a rundown on what you need to think about when meeting with Nastelli. The most important thing to remember, Sabrina, is to have a very open, almost simplistic appearance. You want this guy to think you are a pushover, naïve, and very gullible. You don't want to appear smart, savvy, or doubtful in any way."

Nodding her understanding, she replied, "So dumb-it-down is the way to go?"

"Absolutely. And under no circumstances mention anything about your boyfriend being an ex-SEAL or an investigator."

A blush appeared as she quickly glanced to the side at Jude.

"Right. We got that," Jude interjected, cutting her off before she could reply. He could see her smiling at him, but did not look back over, focusing on the camera instead.

Jack came back on and added, "Luke will get into your virtual accounts—everything from your bank, employment, and even social media. He'll make sure to create the illusion of a very impressionable young woman who will soon be receiving a lot of money from the trust. You'll be the perfect subject for him to become interested in."

At that, both Bart and Jude growled.

Ignoring Bart, Jack said to Jude, "You got a handle on this?"

"Yes, sir," Jude answered back. "Won't deny I hate using Sabrina to get information on how Nastelli works, but yeah…I've got a handle on it."

"We want you to have listening devices so I've put in a call to Jared at his security business. He'll set you up with what you need for this first contact and then we'll get whatever else is needed to you," Jack instructed.

After a few more minutes, the video conference ended leaving Sabrina and Jude alone, staring at each other.

Sighing deeply as he moved toward her, he touched his forehead to hers. "You okay with this?"

She stared into his eyes, seeing the worry lines at the corners. Reaching up, she smoothed them with her fingers. "Yeah, I got this. I'll go talk to Nonnie and let you know when it's set up."

After she left, he pulled up the website of Jack's business. Saints Protection & Investigation. There was no office location listed, but the background picture showed the Blue Ridge Mountains and he remembered Bart talking about where he lived. He thought back to Jack's words, describing his team of employees. *Replicating a team of multi-agency task force. Jesus, that sounds good.*

With a few clicks of his keyboard, he pulled up information on the Blue Ridge area of Virginia. Horse farms, green grass, and mountains in the background. *Beautiful.* He realized he needed to talk to Sabrina sometime soon to see what she thought about the possibility of moving. *Because the thought of working for Jack Bryant's Saints sounded better and better.*

His musings were interrupted by an incoming text.

Nonnie says she can have him for tea tomorrow. OK?

He texted back an affirmative and grinned. The chance to do a little investigative work was just what he needed.

Arlene's longtime housekeeper, Alice, set the tea service on the dark, mahogany coffee table in front of Sabrina before excusing herself, leaving Sabrina with Nonnie and Cecil.

Settled into the comfortable leather sofa with her grandmother to her right, Sabrina had the wireless listening device pinned to her dress, disguised as one of her grandmother's brooches. The jewelry choice was old fashioned, but she hoped it would continue to give the effect of a young woman desperately wanting to please her grandmother in all things.

Sabrina poured the tea, first for her grandmother and then handing a cup to Cecil, sitting in a maroon brocade, wing-back chair. He was clothed in a silk suit. *The grey pin-stripe probably costs more than my rent for several months,* she noted. His black hair was styled and slicked back with gel and his hands, tipped by manicured fingernails, looked as though they had never seen manual labor.

She watched his dark, intelligent eyes as they carefully roamed around the room, assessing everything he saw. She could not determine his age. *Could be forty... could be older.*

Sabrina schooled her expression to be one of complete neutrality, wanting to seem no more than an eager young woman, willing to accept the advice of a medium. Plastering a smile on her face, she said, "I'm hoping you can let us know when you have more information from granddad. Especially in the area of business dealings. It's my understanding that you can ensure his presence can be with us."

"Oh, yes. John's presence is very important to our dear Arlene," Cecil said, offering her a knowing smile. "I have been consulting with John, and have several dates that I think will work for contacting him."

Arlene leaned back in her seat and clapped her hands in glee. "Oh, I knew you could work magic, Cecil."

"Now, now, Arlene. You know this has nothing to do with magic. I am simply a conduit for the ones that have passed on to be able to talk to those still left here."

His cultured voice slithered over Sabrina, causing her to shudder in revulsion. He sipped his tea, comfortable with the delicate china. Sabrina could not help but compare him to Jude and Bart; both would be afraid of holding a cup so breakable in their large paws. A grin threatened to appear, but she squelched it appropriately, focusing back on Cecil.

"Oh, yes I know," Arlene said, bobbing her perfectly coiffed hair. She looked over at Sabrina, saying, "Isn't it wonderful, that we can have John involved in the business again."

Sabrina offered her grandmother a soft smile but found herself recoiling from Cecil. Once more adopting a simplistic expression, she asked, "So what do you have for us?"

"Well, I would need to talk to John some more, but it seems as though he would like to be present before Arlene makes a major financial decision."

Eyes wide, Sabrina exclaimed, "That's fascinating. I never knew a deceased man was able to make financial decisions!"

Chuckling, Cecil admitted, "Well, not directly, of course. But many find that after years of their spouses making financial decisions it is overwhelming to take on the task themselves. So I am able to relieve some of the burdens."

"Do you charge for this service?" Sabrina asked, her voice belying her concern.

"You being interested is a vote of confidence. Of course there are those who do not believe, but our loved ones who have passed on still have a great deal to teach us and have a desire to continue to guide us."

She noted he deflected her question about his fees. His smooth smile oozed over her and she wanted to immediately go home and shower. "I'm still curious about the process," she insisted politely, taking another sip of tea and hoping she did not gag in the process.

Arlene leaned forward and placed her hand on

Cecil's arm. "My granddaughter is very smart and I cannot deny her a chance to learn from her grandfather."

Cecil leaned forward, his eyes boring into Sabrina's. "Yes, I understand you want to have your own business?"

Shrugging, Sabrina giggled. "I work for a small interior design business, but hope to branch out on my own. Of course, I just like making pretty things...I don't really understand the business end." Inwardly cringing at her words, she hoped she was making herself sound gullible without making him suspicious.

"Excellent. That's wonderful. I'm sure your grandfather would love to assist you. I also know that you'll be receiving money from a trust soon. Something set up by your grandfather before he passed?"

"That's true. She's been wondering how best to invest the money in a way that would make her grandfather proud," Arlene answered.

"I'm sure I can help you," he said.

"You?" she said, adopting a wide-eyed, hopeful expression.

"Well, it will be your grandfather's help and I will just be the conduit that reveals his desires."

"And your fees?" she asked again.

"Ah, I see you are a shrewd business woman."

She beamed encouragingly, hoping he would continue.

"I will hold meetings with you and your grandmother, along with John's presence, and advise you on financial matters. Then, when you are satisfied that

John's instructions have been revealed, I ask for a small remuneration. Just to cover my expenses, of course. I would never try to make money off of helping others."

So that's his angle, Sabrina thought. *Wonder how many other rich, elderly women he's fleeced? And now trying it with Nonnie. And me? Hell, no!*

"I think that sounds completely fascinating, Mr. Nastelli," Sabrina said in her best conciliatory voice. "I'd love to be included as well."

She caught the quick flash of excitement in Cecil's eyes before it was immediately replaced with practiced indifference.

"I think that could be arranged. Do you have investments you are interested in?"

"I don't know anything about investments," she answered noncommittally.

Leaning back in his seat, crossing his legs and sipping congenially on his tea, Cecil looked every bit the lord of the manor. "Then I see a very profitable arrangement with Arlene's lovely family and friends."

Jude, parked outside Arlene's home in case something went wrong, listened to the conversation as he recorded it. His jaw was tight with anger, feeling his teeth would crack from his grimace. *Oh, you're gonna find out just how profitable we are, asshole.*

"Oh my God!" Sabrina screamed as she entered Jude's apartment later.

Anxiously awaiting her return, Jude looked up from

his computer. He had listened to the meeting but wanted her opinion of what she had seen. He had been in contact with Bart and Luke, looking at the preliminary information on Nastelli and it was not positive.

Setting his laptop to the side, he watched as Sabrina tossed her keys and purse on the counter before blowing into the room, plopping down on the sofa next to him. He then watched as she jerked her hairpin out allowing the fancy twist of her silky, auburn hair to fall down around her shoulders. The corner of his mouth quirked up as she continued to rant as she kicked off her pumps and unfastened the top two buttons on her demure dress. Throwing her peach-tipped toes up on the coffee table, she leaned back heavily. *She's gorgeous when she's pissed!*

Dragging his eyes back to her flushed face, he said, "I take it The Great Mr. Nastelli meeting did not go well."

Rolling her eyes at the same time an unladylike snort emanated from her was the response.

He scooted over to her and said, "Turn." Watching with pleasure as she immediately acquiesced, he slid his hands over her shoulders and down her back in a massaging motion, feeling some of the tension slide from her. "So, tell me about him."

"You know, I had no idea what he was going to be like. But I hated the oily, slick way he spoke to Nonnie. It was slow, patient, and utterly condescending."

"I heard what he was saying but was dying to be able to watch everything."

"He did pull out a notebook when he started asking Nonnie about what were granddad's favorite months and then dates. Asking when granddad liked to do business transactions so that he can know when best to reach granddad." She ran her hand through her hair before adding, "Good grief, if he's such a great medium and can *talk* to granddad, then he should already know that information!"

Jude laughed, pulling her close. "Glad you can keep your humor, babe."

Turning, she melted into his embrace, burying her face into his chest. The feel of his arms around her brought not only comfort...but peace. *Finally.* Looking up into his strong face, she could not help but run her fingers through his curls, giving them a little tug. "I loved the military look on you, but I have to confess...I love your hair."

"Is that the only thing you love about me, babe?" he asked, his voice already rough with need, his blue eyes meeting hers as his fingers slid through her tresses. The reddish-brown colors glistened in the light.

"Um mm," she purred. "I love everything."

"I'm more than willing to take your mind off of Nastelli," he replied, drawing her up from the couch and touching his forehead to hers. "More than willing." This time, he punctuated his words with his hips pressing his erection into her stomach.

No longer able to contain the smile, she lifted up on her toes as her hand drifted down to palm his crotch. "You got it, sailor-boy."

With one quick swoop, she was in his arms as he stalked toward the bedroom. And for the rest of the night, he worked to erase the case from her mind.

The evening lights cast a shimmery glow over the water, while the dark warehouses cast shadows on the wharf. Without the daytime hustle and bustle of the workers, the area appeared serene. The setting sun had engulfed the horizon with brilliant colors that now gave way to the dark blues of the impending night. The few men gathered hardly noticed. At least Cecil was not paying attention to the scenery.

"I'm getting it. I told you that what I'm working on will give me the money to pay him back." Sweat trickled down his back, soaking his shirt.

"It had better. Mr. Krustas is not in the habit of providing charity."

"I know, I know. I have to play this right. I can't rush this," Cecil growled, hating the intimidation tactics.

"Mr. Krustas isn't interested in what you do. Or how you do it. Only that you pay him back what you borrowed...with interest."

Grimacing, Cecil nodded before turning on his expensive shoes and walking away. Frustration mixed with a hint of fear flowed off of him. As he walked away, staring up at the warehouses, another plan flitted through his mind before slowly taking root. One involving the lovely granddaughter. Slowing his steps, he allowed the alternate plan to form in his mind. *It would be too risky...unless there's no other way. Yes, yes. That's what I'll do. Stick with my plan, unless...*

After he was gone, the two men looked at each

other. The shorter, bulky man asked, "You think he's gonna be a problem. You think he can pull it off?"

"He's done it before but may be taking risks now." Shaking his head, he smirked. "Doesn't matter to me, one way or the other. He either pays what he owes or he goes away. Dumb fuck." Smiling, he turned and walked back into the warehouse, his footsteps echoing in the dark, cavernous space.

7

Sitting in Nonnie's living room again, Sabrina worked hard to hide her disgust. Cecil and Arlene sat next to each other in matching wing-backed chairs, with Sabrina and Ruth opposite them on a plush sofa.

Alice walked in, setting the tea service on the coffee table before looking to her mistress to see what she should do.

"Thank you, Alice," Arlene spoke. "I can serve the tea."

Nodding politely, Alice moved silently from the room, casting a slight disparaging glance toward Cecil. Sabrina leaned forward, reaching for the teapot. "I'll serve, Nonnie," she said, gaining a smile from her grandmother and while noticing that Cecil looked over in acknowledgment. *I'm doing this for Nonnie, not you, you prick!* Schooling her expression, she focused on pouring the tea.

"I've been feeling John so close lately," Cecil said, as

Arlene smiled widely. "I think he will soon be able to tell us what he wants you to do."

Sabrina watched the man with veiled contempt, forcing a simplistic smile on her face once more. He was wearing a different silk suit, the handkerchief perfectly folded in his front pocket and his tie in place with a gold collar bar. From his hair, once again impeccably slicked back, to his highly polished leather shoes, he looked to the casual observer to be a man with expensive taste and the money to indulge his desires. *Jerk!*

Cecil turned his attention to Sabrina, saying smoothly, "With you coming into your trust in a few weeks, do you still want to use the money to finance your new design business."

Sabrina, eyes wide in innocence, breathed, "Oh yes, I'd like to be my own boss."

"That sounds...admirable, but my dear, it takes years for a new business to take off and during that time, your money is just drifting away."

"You know, I think he's right," Arlene said, smiling indulgently at her granddaughter before turning to Cecil. "Is there something else she can do with her money?"

"I'm so glad you asked," Cecil purred. "I know several ventures to invest your money in. The profits will be astronomical and then you'd have all that extra money for your business."

"What does John say about this?" Arlene interjected.

"As I have talked about this with your dear, passed husband, he is definitely in favor of Sabrina investing the money from the trust. As you know, he firmly believed in investing and was well known for his smart financial acuity."

Sabrina watched as Cecil discreetly rubbed the teacup where his fingers handled the delicate china. *He's smudging fingerprints,* she realized, trying to remember everything Jude had told her to watch for. Grateful for the audio equipment that Jude's friend, Jared, had lent to them, she still wished for the visual surveillance that Bart would be bringing soon.

"Oh, yes," Arlene beamed more, looking at Sabrina. "I think you should heed Cecil's advice."

Trying not to explode in anger, Sabrina asked smoothly, "Would you be inclined to share any of granddad's investments advice? I'd very much like to improve my fortune."

"Absolutely," Cecil agreed, his predatory eyes alight with greed.

"How marvelous!" Arlene said, clapping her hands in glee. "John would be so happy."

"Oh, he is," Cecil assured, leaning back in his chair crossing his legs, a smug expression on his face.

"Will you be able to help Ruth as well?" Sabrina asked, wanting to get proof that he was trying to fleece the governor's mother as well.

"Absolutely," Cecil replied, turning to Mrs. Sewell. "Ruth and I have met a few times and I know that her husband used to take John's financial advice when he was living."

"Oh, my. Now that is impressive, isn't it, Sabrina?" Ruth commented, the look of glee on her face matching Arlene's.

"Yes," she agreed, forcing herself to play along when she wanted to scream to her grandmother that she knew he was a phony.

"I'm having a few friends over who are interested in Cecil's ability to gain information from their departed loved ones," Arlene said. "Would you two like to come?"

"Absolutely," Sabrina replied, keeping her expression wide-eyed and naïve.

As the tea party ended and Ruth was leaving, Cecil pushed himself up from his chair. Sabrina's eyes moved to the polished wooden arms. *Bingo! He's left his prints!*

Jude settled in for another phone conference with the Saints. This time, he felt more comfortable in the presence of Jack's other employees as he couched his enthusiasm and methodically went over his report.

"You're doing great," Jack commented, "and I've got to tell you that I spoke to Governor Sewell this morning."

"How'd he take the news?" Jude asked.

"Hell, he wanted to head to Virginia Beach right now to bring his mom back to the Governor's mansion to live," Bart answered.

"As well as wanting to absolutely kick Nastelli's ass," added Cam, a large, smiling, Hispanic man who Bart mentioned recently had come back from a mission in Mexico.

Jack quickly took the conference back in hand, saying, "I've convinced the Governor to not say anything to his mother and to let us continue with our investigation."

Jude realized what was going unsaid. *The governor is counting on me to prove this guy's a swindler!* Recognizing the challenge, he also recognized the opportunity. "What do you need me to do?"

"Bart's driving out tomorrow morning and will outfit you with the equipment you'll need to record what goes on at his grandmother's event. He knows to stay in the background; we don't want Nastelli to get wind that anything is not what it seems. I'll let Luke fill you in on the information he's pulled up for you."

The camera panned around to Luke sitting at his bank of computers, a tall cup of coffee next to him. The dark haired man looked up, nodded his greeting, and said, "I've been digging into this guy and I have to admit that he's good at covering his tracks, but not nearly as good as me." Luke could not hold back the smile as the others chuckled, each knowing he refused to fail at finding out whatever he was looking for.

"Nastelli doesn't have a birth certificate on record so we assume that's not his real name, but I don't know what it is at this point. I compared the data from his modus operandi in Virginia Beach—rich widows, husbands deceased within the last five years, claiming to be a medium, and then getting them to invest in his phony companies. What I've found is there have been a lot of elderly people getting flimflammed in the past years and it's a growing field for con artists. From his physical description, I have possibly matched him to frauds from North Carolina to New York. If it's him, he's gone by Cyril Rosendi, Jorge Carlotta, and a few other that I think are him. So far, I have Rosendi with one arrest years ago, scamming elderly couples into paying for their funeral expenses with a phony company. The other names come up from victims making statements to the police after they've been scammed. Since then, he's been out of the system. Right now, it looks like he's probably made hundreds of thousands of dollars taking lots of grandma's pensions."

"There's more," Jack warned.

"It appears that if he's who we think he is, then he's got ties to Russian mafia in the eastern states. There's no proof, but we need to find a link. Don't know what his involvement is, but nonetheless it makes him more dangerous."

Jude sucked in a breath, his hand running over his hair in his usual frustrated motion. "Not happy about Sabrina doing this."

"Neither are we, so don't do anything else until Bart gets there with the video surveillance equipment. I'm talking to Jared this afternoon to make sure you have his backup as well."

Jude nodded as he watched the mafia report download onto his computer. Looking up, he said, "Okay. Tell me what you need so that we can nail this guy."

Sabrina hugged Bart as he walked into her apartment, glad to see her cousin once more. Right behind her was

Jude, waiting for her to release Bart before he could step in to welcome him as well.

"Good to see you, man. Come on in."

Sabrina moved to the kitchen to grab a few beers and headed back to the living room, not wanting to miss any of their planning conversation.

"How're you doin'?" Bart asked. The dark circles under Sabrina's eyes were evident, but her expression as she looked at Jude was just as telling.

"We're great," she smiled, sitting next to Jude on the sofa. "I confess that this mess with Nonnie wakes me up at night. I just get so mad—"

"Down tiger," Jude whispered, wrapping his arm around her shoulders, grinning at Bart. "You two have the Taggart temper, although it must come from your grandfather's side of the family, 'cause Arlene sure doesn't have it."

Bart laughed, eyeing the pair across from him. "Yeah, I was talking to my dad last night and he was pissed as hell about what Nonnie's doing."

"But it's not her fault, Bart," Sabrina protested. "She's just so lonely without granddad and falling prey to this...this...charlatan!"

"Now that's a term I haven't heard," Jude laughed.

Sabrina shot the two men a fierce glare, saying, "Well, I'm trying to be polite!"

"*Fuckin' asshole* is what I'd call him," Bart replied.

"Yeah, me too," muttered Sabrina, settling back against Jude as she allowed his body to ease her distress.

Jude leaned forward and plucked a plastic bag off the

coffee table. Smiling he handed it to Bart. "Got prints for you."

"Hot damn!" Bart exclaimed, looking at Jude for an explanation.

"He was very careful to wipe his prints off of his teacup, but Sabrina noticed he pushed himself up from his chair when he stood. And the chair had wooden arms. Since she knew Arlene's housekeeper probably polishes the furniture all the time, she figured there would only be his prints on the chair. She contacted me and I told her how to use tape to lift them."

"Perfect," Bart said. "This'll give us the proof to at least tie this guy into the other scams that Luke thinks is him. I'll get this to Monty and his FBI contacts." Turning back to the pair, he said, "Tell me about this meeting Nonnie's got going?"

"Tomorrow afternoon she's having a small gathering of people interested in what Nastelli has to say about investing the way John thinks is good. The governor's mother is coming, plus two other wealthy widows from what I can tell. Sabrina will be there as well and I'll be outside listening and watching."

"He's gonna do a séance?" Bart asked incredulously.

"Don't know how he's gonna do it, but supposedly the time is right for John to speak to him. My guess is that he's gonna suggest investments in phony companies or ones where he can get hold of their money."

"What can we do to make sure that doesn't happen?" Sabrina asked.

Bart grinned, confessing, "Well, we've made sure he won't be taking advantage of Nonnie or Mrs. Sewell."

Seeing Jude and Sabrina's questioning expressions, he added, "Luke has hacked into their bank and investments accounts and...um...let's just say there's a hold right now."

Sabrina's eyebrows shot upward in surprise. "Is that legal?"

"Cuz, you don't need to worry about that. Just focus on your part tomorrow," Bart said, with a laugh.

Huffing, she rolled her eyes. "I've got this. Even if I have to bite my tongue the whole time, I'll play my part perfectly."

Jude, wanting to move forward in the planning, said, "Jack said you'd have some equipment for me?"

Back to business, Bart leaned forward pulling open the small duffel bag he had carried inside with him. He pulled out equipment that was familiar to Jude and completely foreign to Sabrina. "Here's a wireless device for video recording. You'll wear this to the meeting and it will not only record the conversation, but we'll be listening and watching it as well. Keep him talking. Keep him at ease. At our meeting yesterday we discussed the psychology of the con-artist. He's smart and he'll pick up on someone who doubts what he's doing." Bart cast a stern look at Sabrina, saying, "So you gotta convince him that whatever granddad's telling him is the most important thing to you."

She nodded, understanding what her cousin was saying. "I can do this. Knowing how important this is for Nonnie, I'll be perfect. I promise."

With a nod, Bart continued. "Right. Okay, what we need is for Nastelli to give us company names. Specifics.

Not just talk in general terms, 'cause there's nothing wrong with that. If he's actually hustling to get money into phony companies that he has titles to, then we've got him for fraud."

Both Jude and Sabrina nodded their agreement.

"And while you two are getting evidence recorded from whatever Nastelli is *revealing*," he said sarcastically, "I'll be at his place, seeing what I can discover!"

At that, Sabrina's eyebrows shot up once more. "Now I know that's not legal!" She glanced at Jude and when she saw his unsurprised expression, she realized that however Bart did his job, it must be what was expected. *And that's what Jude will be doing if he works for one of the investigation businesses.* She lost track of what the two men were discussing for a moment as she pondered Jude's new career. Glancing back over at his face, she watched as he listened attentively to Bart. Focused. His expression grim, but intent. And his eyes... she could see the interest and life in his eyes. *This is what he was meant to do. The SEALs first...and now this.*

"Babe?" Jude said, drawing her out of her reverie.

"Sorry," she said, blinking rapidly. "I was lost in thought."

"You okay?" Jude asked gently, pulling her body back into his.

Smiling, first at him and then Bart, she said, "Yeah. I was just...um...well, to be honest, I was thinking about the job that you two are doing. Kind of...unusual...but you both seem to enjoy it."

"Hell, yeah," Bart replied. "I love the investigation side of what I do and Jude's a natural." Bart leaned back, taking a pull on his beer. "And when it's personal like this...it's a fuckin' great feeling taking down some asshole who's hurting someone you care about."

Bart reached back into his bag and pulled out a small, flat disk. I talked to Jack and since you're involved, and while we hope nothing bad will happen, we've got a tracer for you to wear."

"A tracer?"

"Yeah, this way we can find you if anything goes wrong." Seeing her wide eyes looking up in fear, he quickly said, "Jude'll be right outside of Nonnie's house, so nothing can happen. But I'd rather be safe than sorry."

"Hell, yeah," Jude agreed.

"Now, I just need some kind of necklace that this will attach to. Do you have a pendant that'll work?"

Sabrina's mind quickly ran through the necklaces she owned but could not come up with one that would fit the tracer disc.

"Here, babe. Use this," Jude insisted, pulling his St. Jude medallion from around his neck.

Bart stared at the necklace for a moment, surprise in his expression, then shook his head, taking it from Jude's hands. Quickly attaching the tracer, he handed it back to Jude, who slipped it over Sabrina's head and settled the medallion between her breasts.

"The Patron Saint of the impossible?" she asked softly.

Chuckling, Jude replied, "Yeah. I'm beginning to think that now that you're back in my life, nothing's impossible."

The trio sat in companionable silence for a minute, sipping their beers, each to their own thoughts, before Bart spoke again. "My parents were solid. My dad is like granddad—smart, intuitive, and worked hard in what he knew he could do. Mom is more emotional, but dad keeps her grounded. I miss granddad like crazy, but I know it's nothing compared to what Nonnie feels." He took another sip, letting his memories slide over him. "I can't stand the idea that someone is trying to hurt her using granddad's memory."

Sabrina leaned forward, placing her hand on his leg. "I know, Bart. I feel the same."

Bart pinned Jude with a stare, saying, "I deal in what I can investigate and this mumbo-jumbo shit that Nastelli's got Nonnie believing? Not for me, and it makes my blood boil that someone can pretend to talk to the dead to take advantage of others who still grieve. If I could shut down every psychic, medium, mind-reader, bogus shit-head con-artist, I would!"

"Don't hold anything back, cousin!" Sabrina laughed, easing the tension.

Shaking his head, Bart chuckled. "Yeah, guess I get a little carried away."

"No worries, man," Jude acknowledged. "But we've got this for tomorrow. You get into his place, I'll be outside of Arlene's watching and listening while Sabrina gets him talking and recorded. And hopefully, after tomorrow, Nastelli will go down!"

With a nod between the three, they settled back in their seats, finally able to enjoy the afternoon.

8

Jude seemed pre-occupied that evening, so Sabrina was determined to give him some space. She wandered back into the kitchen to grab a beer for him and a glass of wine for her. Her eyes glanced to the refrigerator door, covered in photographs she had printed of the two of them, taken ever since they had met. Even when just friends, she had been determined to record their relationship. *We don't have kids yet and I've already decorated the refrigerator! Kids. Oh, God, I hope he wants kids.*

Remembering the first time she lay eyes on him, her mind drifted back in time. Tall, muscular, blue-grey eyes, and oh, so handsome. Her cousin had wanted to meet up with his former commander and they were invited to a backyard party. The yard was filled with SEALs and there was no shortage of tall, handsome, and very sexy. Even her gorgeous, blond cousin was every woman's fantasy. But for her, as soon as her eyes hit Jude's, she was lost.

As he had walked over, she needed to lean her head

back to keep her gaze on his face. *But it wasn't just his face I was looking at.* He had been in the process of pulling his t-shirt over his head. His ripped abs were lick-worthy as they led down to his low-slung cargo shorts. She remembered thinking as he pulled his shirt back down what a waste it was to keep that chest covered.

She could tell he was interested but quickly ascertained that his reticence was because she was with Bart. As soon as she could, she had let it be known Bart was her cousin. And in no time at all, Jude staked his claim.

Inseparable between his missions, she was more than willing to wait for him whenever he got home. When he was injured, she was not sure they would survive as he continually pushed her away, but she refused to give up on him or on them.

Lost in thought, she jumped when his arms encircled her waist from behind. Squeaking, she whirled around, a smile quickly replacing her surprise.

"Who were you expecting?" he joked.

"You are so quiet, you can be quite the sneak," she said as he pulled her body closer. As her breasts pressed into his chest, she gently rocked her hips forward, feeling his erection against her pelvis.

"I was wondering what you were so preoccupied with earlier, but now it seems as though you have worked out all your demons," she giggled, her arms tightening around his waist.

Leaning back to look into her face, he said, "I'm sorry, babe. I didn't mean to be poor company."

"Anything you want to talk about?" she offered.

With another push of his erection against her body, he admitted, "Not right now. Only one thing on my mind now." With that, he leaned down and took her mouth. The kiss started slow, tasting the wine on her lips. As he took the kiss deeper, he swallowed her moan as his tongue explored the warm crevices. Her arms lifted above her head as he moved his hands to the bottom of her t-shirt and pulled it off, tossing it to the kitchen floor.

Her hands went to her tight, black yoga pants, hooking her thumbs into the waistband and sliding them down as far as she could without letting go of the kiss. Kicking her legs back and forth, she managed to release her pants and panties, letting them fall onto the floor next to her blouse. Next she reached for his belt, but he pulled away.

"Uh unh," he said. "I was such poor company earlier I'm making it up to you now. This is about you." With that, he lifted her up on the kitchen counter then slid his hands up her back, unsnapping her bra. It also landed on the floor.

She watched as he dipped his head, kissing his way from her lips to her earlobe, then down where her pulse beat erratically in her neck. She leaned back, propping herself up with her hands on the counter behind her, thrusting her naked breasts forward.

Not one to turn down an invitation from his beautiful girlfriend, he latched onto one nipple pulling it hard into his mouth. Alternating between sucking, licking, and nipping gently with his teeth, he had her squirming on the counter, desperate to have him buried deep inside of her.

Moaning, she grabbed his shoulders pulling his face away from her breasts, and shouted, "Jude! Stop playing and get to business!"

Grinning his panty melting grin, he fussed, "Now, now, darlin'. You have to be patient."

He slid his hands down her legs to her cute blue-painted toenails and threw her legs over his shoulders. *Blue,* he grinned. *That's a new color.* Kneeling down, his face at her core, all thoughts of her pretty toes left his head as his hands pulled her forward so that her sex was right on the edge of the counter.

"This, babe, is the prize," he said, licking her before nipping at her clit.

"Oh, my God," she moaned once more. "DBO!"

He stopped for a moment, looking up at her face in confusion. "DBO?"

She dropped her head back down, smiling into his face. "Yeah, honey. It's what you do to me all the time. Death by orgasm."

Laughing, he nodded, saying, "DBO. I like it."

"Well, so do I, so get back to it sailor-boy," she demanded.

"Yes, ma'am," he agreed, dropping back down to plunge his tongue into her wet folds. While his tongue worked magic between her legs, his hands moved upwards, lifting and palming her full breasts.

He loved her natural breasts from the first time he saw her in the sundress. It seemed that an unusual number of the women hanging around in the bars near the Naval base had implants. He had not minded at the time. As far as he was concerned, boobs were boobs. But once he had his hands on hers, nothing else would do. Sabrina's perfect C-cup? *Fuckin' beautiful!*

Within a few minutes, she was squirming on the counter, begging for her release. He moved up to suck her clit deeply while pinching both nipples. With a scream, she threw her head back and cried out his name as the orgasm overtook her. The electric shocks jolted from her core outwards, leaving her limp and breathless.

Grinning in male satisfaction, Jude stood back up and licked his lips, wet from her juices. Picking her up in his arms, he carried her toward the bedroom. *Thank God I can do this again,* remembering the time not too long ago when he was unable to lift her and walk. That simple act alone was one of the reasons he pushed himself so hard in physical therapy, even after knowing that he would not be returning to his team.

He debated on whether or not to toss her onto the bed or lay her down gently, but before he could make up his mind, she grabbed his cheeks, pulling him in, latching onto his lips.

Plunging her tongue into his mouth, she dove in tasting the essence of both of them. His arms could not let go of her luscious body, so the decision was made as he lay her down on the bed, his body covering hers.

"You have on entirely too many clothes," she mumbled between kisses, trying to lift his shirt.

Nipping her lips, he stood up from the bed and lifted his shirt over his head. She leaned up on her elbows and watched as the muscles in his abs and arms moved. He was perfectly sculpted—an Adonis of a man.

He slid his belt out of his jeans and watched as her eyes lit up once his fingers began unzipping. Dropping his pants and boxers, he palmed his engorged cock. "You want this, babe?"

Her gaze, which had not wavered from his hips, shot up as she looked into his face. Smiling, she nodded. "Oh, yeah. You know I do."

"What do you want me to do with this?" he teased.

Licking her lips, she debated whether she wanted to take him in her mouth or have him deep inside. The need for him buried was overpowering, so she replied, "Just fuck me, please."

"Darlin', you don't have to beg," he grinned as he leaned over her. Grasping her legs in his hands, he lifted her knees back toward her as he moved in for the perfect angle. Setting his cock at her entrance he pushed to the hilt, the feel of her tight sex grabbing his cock almost undoing him immediately. Using his ability to control his body from years as a SEAL, he forced himself to enjoy the ride and make sure she came again.

She watched him with hooded eyes, his chest muscles moving with each thrust. His powerful arms held himself above her, his smooth shoulders held tightly in her grip. It did not take long in this position, where she was so exposed. Every thrust ground his pelvis against her sensitive clit and she swore she was about to fly apart.

His gaze dropped from her flushed face to her breasts, bouncing with each thrust, to where their bodies were joined. He heard the noises she made when her orgasm was about to overtake her and he lifted his gaze back to her face, a satisfied smile on his lips.

Her head slammed back onto the mattress as he shifted once more on her clit and cried out in pleasure as the electric jolt sent tremors throughout her body. As he leaned down and grasped a distended nipple in his mouth, sucking hard, she felt the orgasm last longer than she ever remembered. Just when she did not imagine she could take any more, she felt him elongate inside and knew that he was about to follow her in bliss.

With his neck muscles corded and veins standing out, he roared through his orgasm, thrusting over and over until the last drop had been wrung out of him. Falling down to her side, he gathered her in his arms. Chest to chest, heartbeat to heartbeat.

It took several minutes for either one of them to speak, their sated bodies lying on the bed in a tangle of arms and legs.

As the euphoria slowly passed and their heart rates slowed, he gently moved out of bed with her in his arms. Carrying her to the bathroom, he cleaned her off before carrying her back. Tucking her into his side, they lay in the dark room, the moon casting shadows all around.

After a few minutes, Sabrina asked, "Sweetie?"

"Right here, babe."

"Can you tell me what you were thinking earlier?"

A moment of silence passed and she began to think that he was not going to answer.

Sucking in a deep breath and letting it out slowly, he said, "I was thinking about my job."

She stayed silent, knowing he needed to take his time to let her know what he was thinking. She knew he was dissatisfied at work and just wanted him to be happy.

"I've lived near the beach for a long time. This was my fun place, my career, and my calling. As a SEAL, it was where I wanted to be. But, babe, I've been thinking lately that maybe it was time to get away from the beach."

Confusion spread across her face. "Like a vacation?" she asked.

"No, more like a permanent move."

"What?" she said, sitting up quickly, drawing the sheet up to cover herself. "You want to leave? You want to move away from me?" Her voice rose with each word.

"No, no!" he said, scooting up against the headboard and turning on the bedside lamp so he could see her face clearly. Gathering her into his arms, he settled her against his body, his arms enveloping her. "I'm sorry, babe. I didn't mean I wanted to move away from you. I just thought maybe we could move somewhere else and start over. A place where I'm not constantly reminded what I don't have and, well...somewhere you don't have to always deal with your grandmother."

She could not help but bite her lip in thought. She loved Nonnie, but her grandmother would often remark to Sabrina that she did not need to work, still thinking that her interest in interior design was more of a hobby than a career. Jude knew that she longed to break away from the constricting viewpoint that Nonnie expressed. He always said he did not care that her family had money, after all, she lived off of her own salary.

He noticed she was quiet, so he lifted her so she was straddling his lap. "Babe, you get me, don't you? This has nothing to do with you. This is me, feeling like I need a break from always running into SEALs and that's exactly what I would be doing if I stayed at my job or if I go work for Jared."

She nodded her understanding and asked, "So what would you like to do? Or where would you like to go?"

"I want to take Jack up on his offer to work with the Saints Protection and Investigations. But I'd need to move to somewhere near his base."

She leaned in for a gentle kiss and whispered against his lips, "Wherever you go, that's where home will be. We just have to figure out our future...together."

Once more, thanking his lucky stars for finding a woman like Sabrina, he rolled her over and made love to her again. This time slow. Easy. Full of promises.

Cecil sat in his condo looking out over the Chesapeake Bay. The blue sky reflected on the diamond water, but the spectacular scene was lost on him. His mind was on the next day...channeling John Taggart for his gullible widow. *Channeling?* The snort escaped as he thought about the woman playing right into his hands. *And the pretty granddaughter?* Just as naive.

Scribbling on a pad of paper, he quickly figured out how much he needed from each of them to pay off his debt to Krustas and have enough to start over somewhere else. *Maybe Florida next time. There are tons of wealthy widows there.*

The phone rang and he was tempted to not answer it. Rubbing his hand over his unkempt hair, he sighed heavily, glancing at the number displayed. *Got to answer...no choice.*

"Yes," he answered brusquely.

"Two days. That was the agreement and in two days, your time is up."

"I've got this, I tell you. Tomorrow I'll be able to pay everything back. I'll get the money tomorrow. Then I'll deposit it and come straight there," Cecil promised.

"Mr. Krustas doesn't care how you get it. Only that you are here with the money within two days."

"I don't appreciate threats," Cecil growled, his shaking voice belying his false bravado.

"Krustas does not make threats," came the smooth, unruffled reply. "Only promises."

9

The next afternoon Sabrina perched on the rose settee in her grandmother's parlor. Across from her sat two of Arlene's friends, and from their appearances they seemed to fit the wealthy widow mark that Mr. Nastelli was looking for. While the women smiled and chatted, Sabrina noticed a nervous anxiety among them. *Wanting to please. Wanting to believe that a deceased husband would talk to Cecil and give them direction. Wanting to feel that connection once more.* The realization of the type of prey he worked on angered her once more, but she continued to have a simplistic smile on her face, hoping to keep him in the dark as to her true intent.

Sabrina noticed her grandmother was serving the tea instead of her housekeeper. "Nonnie? Where's Alice today?"

"Cecil said that we needed to have all possible unbelievers out of the house so I gave her the day off."

Perched delicately on another chair was Ruth

Sewell, her eyes bright with anticipation, hands fluttering nervously, chatting with Arlene. And Cecil was sitting in a comfortable, winged back chair, lording over the proceedings. After tea had been served and the conversation died down, all eyes turned to him expectantly.

Smiling benevolently, Cecil leaned forward, "My dears," he began. "You know why we are here. It is time," he said, drawing his words out dramatically, "to talk to John and discover what he wants to reveal to us."

He stood and moved to the heavy drapes in the room, closing them so that the afternoon sun was completely shut out. The only light in the room came from the few table lamps he left lit. Sabrina shifted nervously, hoping the video and audio recording device was working properly.

"Oh, please let's talk to John," Arlene begged.

"I think that's a good plan," Cecil agreed and moved to sit directly across from her. He crossed his feet and took her hands in his. "Are you ready?"

"Yes, indeed," she replied.

"Now, remember ladies. This is not like what you see on TV. There will be no voices coming at you, no ghosts walking around, no scary lights or sounds. I am a true medium and the deceased come to me. I can hear them and then I interpret what they are saying to you."

The ladies all leaned in anxiously, hanging on his every word. Sabrina found herself doing exactly what they did, her anxiety notching upward. *Boy, he's smooth,* she thought as she realized she was also eagerly anticipating what would come.

Cecil sat perfectly straight, his eyes closed as he lifted his hands, palms up. Humming softly, he began to chant as he swayed slowly back and forth.

"John is with us, Arlene," he said, his silky voice soothing. Nodding, his expression did not change for a moment as he appeared to be listening.

Sabrina caught her grandmother's gaze and smiled in encouragement. She hated pretending but knew it was the only way to prove him false.

"He loved Christmas," Cecil said. "He's telling me how much he enjoyed spending money on his family."

"Oh, yes," Arlene enthused.

"Giving you the diamond brooch the first year he turned a profit in his business. The video games when the grandchildren were small. And...ah, the trip to the Bahamas for your twenty-fifth anniversary."

Sabrina noted the other women watched with rapt attention on both Cecil and Arlene's obvious approval. Sabrina could not stop the pounding of her heart as her eyes darted to him, seeking the secret to his control.

"You *are* talking to him. Oh, please tell him I miss him," Arlene said, tears forming in her eyes.

"He knows, my dear. He knows."

"Sabrina?" Cecil, with his eyes still closed, addressed her. "He says he is proud of you. Proud of wanting to start your own business, but he does not think it is wise to sink all of your money in a new business. You need to invest, so that your money grows."

Cecil continued to sway as he nodded for several more minutes. "Ladies, he has given me his recommendations for investments. He says this is the perfect time to strike while the iron is hot."

Ruth Sewell, eyes alight, nodded. "Oh, my husband always said that the beginning of the month was a good time to look at our money."

"Yes," Cecil smiled. "John says that your husband was a good friend. He remembers the last time they played golf at the Seaside Golf Resort. Yes, he says you would do well to heed his advice."

"Tell me what to do," Ruth demanded.

Cecil lifted his hand to silence her as he continued to sway gently. Finally giving a nod, he leaned back in his chair and opened his eyes. Wiping his brow, he turned his gaze toward Arlene. "May I trouble you for a drink, dear Arlene? I find the process to be exhausting."

The elderly women immediately began to fuss over him, irritating Sabrina even more. She stayed very still, hoping the miniature camera she was wearing was capturing the scene. *Please, just let us get enough to catch this rat.*

Jude sat across the street from Arlene's house, the video and audio feeding directly into his laptop, watching the proceedings. He wished he could see Sabrina, knowing it was impossible since she was wearing the surveillance equipment, but he had to admit she was doing brilliantly. Glancing at the computer, he knew that Jack's business had the money and the contacts to take on cases like this that would either go by the wayside or get buried in red-tape. They also took on government contracts that would send him on missions where his SEAL rescue training would come in handy. Smiling to himself, he confirmed in his mind, *this is it. This is my future. And with Sabrina with me—*

His attention was once more riveted to the monitor as it appeared the meeting was breaking up. Cecil walked back to the windows and opened the curtains, allowing the bright, afternoon sun to shine in. Jude watched as the women blinked their eyes, blinded by both the light and the idea of gaining financial insight from Arlene's husband through Cecil.

He listened as Sabrina asked about the investments. *Come on, asshole. Give me something to nail you with.* Luke was on standby, listening and watching the same feed as Jude, and as soon as Nastelli took money for phony companies, they would have the evidence needed to turn him over to the FBI.

"Now ladies, I do not actually do the investing. But my associates are financial investors who will place your money in the companies that John has told me he believes will reap the greatest rewards."

"What are some of the companies that granddad recommends," Sabrina asked with wide-eyed innocence, playing her part perfectly.

Cecil rattled off the names of several companies as Sabrina and the other women nodded as though the names meant something to them.

Jude quickly sent a note to the Saints, knowing that

Luke would check the companies. *Bet they're phony set-ups with Nastelli as the sole proprietor,* he thought.

Jude watched as Sabrina kept her body aimed directly at Nastelli, so the video was perfect. The women all approached the table, checkbooks in hand.

"Who do we make the checks out to?" Sabrina asked, her voice full of eager innocence.

"The easiest thing to do is write them to me, and I will contact my investors immediately. I will turn the money over to them by this afternoon," Cecil assured.

Jude watched as the women began writing checks. *Got him!*

Jack called him immediately. "Sabrina was great. We've got the evidence for Monty to feed to his FBI contact, who's on alert right now. They'll watch him and so will Luke. As soon as he deposits the money into his personal account, they'll move in."

"Good, cause I want Sabrina out of this!"

"Okay, once she's out of the house, let us know. Bart should be reporting in, letting us know what he sees in Nastelli's condo. Then we'll stay in touch with the FBI and the Governor's office."

Bart moved stealthily through Cecil's condo apartment, smiling at the ease with which he was able to break into the expensive, but lax security, building. His years as a Navy SEAL gave him the ability to move covertly and the confidence to know he was smarter than the asshole he was stalking. As his gaze swept the space, he noted the few pieces of basic furniture and lack of decoration. *Looks like a man who's not planning on putting down roots.* His observations were confirmed when he moved to the bedroom, seeing Nastelli's clothes already packed in a suitcase. *Slick-shit is probably hoping to get checks today from the women and then hit the road.*

Seeing nothing else of interest there, he headed over to the table, covered in magazines and newspaper clippings. Scanning quickly, he saw they were prints of the local newspaper with old and recent articles about John and Arlene Taggart. One had a newspaper article of John and Ruth Sewell's husband playing golf. Another showed his grandparents coming back from a cruise. One article was on a local jewelry store, picturing Arlene with a diamond brooch.

A laptop was open and Bart deftly searched the history, once more finding searches concerning the Taggarts and Sewells. Sabrina's name caught his eye and he recognized that Nastelli had been doing his homework on her as well. *Not very original,* he thought, *but when dealing with lonely, naïve persons, I guess it doesn't take much to convince them that someone still wants to take care of them.*

Doing a search with Sabrina's name on the computer, Bart wanted to see what else Nastelli had tried to find on his cousin. Her name appeared on the email lists. Clicking, he scanned them, a red haze of anger blinding him. *It seemed that Nastelli might have had other plans for his cousin than just fleecing her out of her trust.*

Jude watched as Nastelli left in a taxi and the other women had their drivers pick them up. Sabrina walked over and hopped into his car.

"How'd I do?" she asked, her hands nervously shaking.

Leaning over, he kissed her deeply before moving back away. "Babe, you were phenomenal, but I want you out of this now! I've never been nervous about any SEAL mission, but you in there with that slime? Made me fuckin' crazy!"

She giggled and nodded. "I have to admit, this cloak and dagger is not for me. I was a wreck in there, trying to keep my camera pointed his way, wanting to focus on what he said so that I'd know how to respond, and not lose my cool and call him out!"

"Well, this is it, baby. You're done. Luke's got the video feed and they're already watching his bank accounts. Jack's working with the Governor's office and FBI. And Bart should be finished with Nastelli's apartment."

Looking at his watch, he said, "I hate to do this, but I've got to get back to work. Only two more weeks of my severance contract and then I'll be a free man."

Excitement filling her voice, she said, "And then we can look for a place near Jack and Bart?"

"Absolutely," he promised. "Do you want me to drop you off at your apartment?"

"Nah. I think I'll go back inside and sit with Nonnie

for a while. I actually think that all of this has made her miss granddad more."

"Good idea. I'll see you tonight, baby."

He watched her as she re-entered Arlene's house before driving away, never seeing the return of the taxi from the road behind him.

"Jack? Got a problem," Bart growled. "I'm in Nastelli's place and checked his computer. He's definitely involved with organized crime here in the area. He's been borrowing heavily from one of the local bosses in the Russian mafia and they want their money back so he's getting antsy."

"Send me the sites and emails," Luke demanded. "I can figure out who the hell we're dealing with!"

A moment passed while Bart quickly sent everything he could find to Luke's secure computer. While Luke was beginning to work his magic, Jack commented, "There was a Russian mafia family that was busted about six years ago in Virginia Beach."

While Luke was still working on the information Bart had sent, Chad did a search on what Jack had just pronounced. "Yeah, it was all over the news. Twenty-six of them were arrested."

"Another family must have stepped in to take their

place," Bart surmised. "Jesus, there's no shortage of criminals."

There was a pause while Luke continued his search. "Looks like the new kid on the block could be the Krustas family. Although, I will have to say that they've been around for a long time. Probably took advantage six years ago to take over the whole Hampton Road area."

"Well, they're back in force again. I want protection for Sabrina. Nastelli's emails indicate that if he doesn't pay by the end of this week he's a dead man and it seems as though he's considering using Sabrina as collateral if needed. I called Jude and he's heading back over to Nonnie's house where they both are."

"Bingo," Luke called out. "Looks like the Krustas family has had some problems of their own. Old man Krustas came out fine, but he had some family that are now enjoying a long stay at one of the state's finest prisons."

"I'm calling the governor now," Jack growled. "Monty's working on getting the FBI to come search Nastelli's place also. They'll do it legally so let them do their job."

"Right. I'm heading over to Nonnie's also, to finally talk some sense into her head about this shit. It's gone on long enough."

"Got it. You need immediate assistance, get hold of Jared. I'm alerting him as well."

Disconnecting, Bart hustled to his vehicle and headed to his grandmother's house, thoughts of strangling Nastelli going through his head.

Jude had almost made it back to the Naval base when the call came in from Bart. The news that Nastelli was in debt to the Russian mob in the Hampton Roads area ratcheted his concern to an even higher level. Glancing down at the clock, he calculated he and Bart should reach Arlene's house about the same time.

He knew Arlene would hate hearing that her late husband had not really spoken to Cecil, but hopefully with Sabrina and Bart's help, she would be all right.

Trying to call Sabrina, it went straight to voicemail. He remembered Nastelli telling the ladies to make sure they silenced their phones. *Damn – she must have forgotten to turn hers back on.*

"Nonnie?" Sabrina called, as she walked back through the house toward the kitchen. It was her favorite room in the house, although she had to admit that she had wonderful memories of every room. Nonnie had always insisted that she wanted the house to feel warm and inviting, hating the pretentious homes of some of her friends.

The large, airy kitchen was painted a sunny yellow, with green accents. The distressed, white painted cabinets were a perfect backdrop for the white and grey marble countertops. Ever since she had been a little girl, a cookie jar always sat on the counter, filled with treats.

She walked around the kitchen counter, greeting Arlene with a kiss.

"My dear, what brings you back? Did you forget something?"

"No, no. I just thought I'd visit for a while. Are you... feeling okay after all of that?"

"Of course. It was thrilling to know that John is still guiding us."

Sighing deeply as she held her grandmother in a strong embrace, she said, "Nonnie, you have to know that granddad is with us in our hearts all of the time. We don't need someone like Cecil to tell us what granddad would want us to do."

Arlene pulled out of Sabrina's arms, peering deeply into her face. "I know you, Sabrina. You're holding back. What are you trying to say?"

Licking her lips, she looked down at her grandmother's hands clasped in her own before lifting her gaze back to Arlene's face. "Bart and Jude have been investigating Cecil." She felt her grandmother try to pull her hands away, but she held tight. "Please listen to me. They think he's been working with organized crime here and he pretends to talk to the dead so that he can steal money from...um—"

"Foolish old ladies? Is that what you were going to say?"

"No, no! Just...maybe, lonely...vulnerable."

She watched carefully as her grandmother visibly grappled with the news Sabrina shared. "Nonnie, Cecil's good at what he does. That's how he was able to get away with this for so long." Giving a little tug on her hands, she brought Arlene's attention back to her. "But Jude and Bart are better at what they do. I...I was wired today."

"Wired? Whatever does that mean?" Suddenly, Arlene's face showed understanding. "Like with cameras? Like what you see on TV?"

Sabrina pulled the miniature camera, hidden in a pin holding her scarf in place, off her blouse. "They recorded everything and then checked. They're turning the evidence over to the FBI and you've got to know that Ruth's son is furious." She lay the pin on the kitchen counter.

Sabrina saw tears forming in her grandmother's eyes and she pulled her back in for another hug. "Oh, Nonnie. It's going to be okay."

"I've been so foolish. And now I've given him money and encouraged Ruth to do the same."

"Don't worry. Your bank has already been alerted. He won't get any of your money. Nor mine, nor any of the ladies here. When he tries to cash the checks, he won't get anything."

"Well, that's too bad," Cecil's voice growled behind them.

Whirling around, the two women stared at him in surprise. "What are you doing here?" Sabrina asked, instinctively moving in front of her grandmother.

"Seems granny here forgot to sign her check. I noticed the oversight right away but before I could come back in, I saw you get in that car with what had to be a detective."

Sabrina sucked in a gasp of surprise.

"Yeah, you didn't know I saw you. I figured you were up to something so I slipped back in and now I know." His hand reached out to grab the pin from the counter and dropped to the floor where with one stomp of his expensive shoe, he smashed the recording device to bits.

He reached into his jacket pocket pulling out a gun as his eyes darted around

Gasping once more, she held her arms out attempting to shelter her grandmother. "You're upset with me," she said, her voice shaking. "Leave Nonnie out of this."

"Bitch, you're goddamn right I'm mad at you!" He pulled the checks out from his pants pocket throwing them on the floor. "And thanks to you, these are worthless."

Sweating profusely, he no longer held the debonair appearance that was his norm. "They'll kill me if I can't pay them back. I've got to have a plan. I've got to—" Suddenly he stopped pacing and ranting, turning abruptly to face her.

"Taking the old lady won't do me any good, but giving you to them...yeah. I've got no choice. You're a much better hostage. Worth far more than I owed them." Seeming to make up his mind, he grabbed her arm, jerking her forcefully toward him.

"No!" Arlene shouted, with a strength she forgot she had.

Pointing the gun at the two women, he ordered them to the side of the room while he opened a few drawers. Finding duct tape, he threw it at Sabrina.

"Tape her to the chair and be quick about it. And don't try anything, bitch, 'cause I'll check it."

Not knowing what else to do, she followed his instructions. "I'm sorry," she whispered, feeling her grandmother's hands shaking as she taped her to the chair.

"Oh, my dear, this is all my fault. If I hadn't been so intent on trying to connect with your grandfather."

"No, the fault lies squarely on Cecil's shoulders. He's the one to blame," she assured Arlene. Standing, she turned back to him. "It's done."

"Let's go," he ordered, waving the gun toward the door leading to the garage.

"Where are you taking me?" she asked, hoping that if someone found her grandmother, at least she would be able to tell them where she was taken.

"Oh, no, sweetheart. Not in front of the old bat. Come on."

After bending to kiss her grandmother, she moved ahead of him and into the large garage.

"Turn around. Hands behind your back," he ordered. Seeing her hesitation, he grinned, "unless you want me to go back and visit granny."

Pursing her lips, she turned, her mind racing to see if she could somehow overpower him, but he was clever. Keeping the pistol on her with one hand, he used his free hand, crudely wrapping duct tape around her wrists. Once they were taped together, he set the weapon down and wrapped them tightly.

"Get in," he growled, grabbing a set of keys from a

hook near the door before shoving her into the back seat.

"Where are we going?" she asked.

"Got some friends who will take you as the collateral against what I owe. We'll head to the Krustas warehouses on the waterfront in Norfolk."

Krustas? Why does that sound familiar? Suddenly she remembered reading that name in the newspaper earlier in the year. Some members of the Krustas family were arrested in conjunction with a federal sting operation cracking down on illegal smuggling...including human trafficking. *Oh, Jesus. How does he know them?*

Afraid to glance down, she could only pray the tracking device on her St. Jude necklace was working.

Jude pulled up to Arlene's house at the same time that Bart's SUV careened into the driveway. Both men jumped from their vehicles, running to the front door. Finding it unlocked, they powered inside yelling for the women.

Hearing Arlene's voice from the kitchen, they rounded the corner only to find her duct-taped to the chair, tears streaming down her face.

"Nonnie!" Bart shouted as he knelt down, quickly slicing her bonds. "What happened?"

Not seeing Sabrina, Jude turned to rush out of the room, but Arlene's voice brought him to a halt.

"He took her. He's not real. He's a thief and he took her," she cried.

Bart picked her up and stalked to the family room, laying her gently on the sofa. Twisting to Jude, he barked, "Call Jack. Get Luke to pull her up on the tracker." Turning back to his grandmother he quickly assessed determining that she was not injured, just distraught.

Jude, trying to quell his panic while on the phone with the Saints, was assured that Luke was working to find where she was. Running to the garage, he ascertained which vehicle of Arlene's was missing and relayed that to Bart, who was on the phone with the police.

Luke called back. "Looks like she's in Norfolk, heading to the waterfront. Closest warehouses around belong to the Krustas Corporation. We know they're the strongest Russian mafia's presence in Virginia. If he's involved, the FBI will want in on our action. Fuck, they'd love to nail him as well!"

In a split-second decision, Jude hung up and quickly called Jared. "Need help."

"You need it, it's yours. What's up?" Jared replied without hesitation.

"Nastelli's got Sabrina. He found out we were on to him and he's taking her somewhere on the Norfolk waterfront. Jack's man says that the Krustas warehouses are there and they might be—"

"Russian organized crime," Jared finished for him.

"Bart knows where it is and we've got to get there now. Any chance for some assistance?"

"Absolutely. You got it. But I gotta tell you that old man Krustas isn't gonna be happy that Nastelli's bringing her there. He's working to keep the Feds outta his business on the waterfront and while he's not clean, he's gonna be fuckin' pissed to have this brought to his door."

"Is that good news for us?"

"Maybe. You and Bart get down there. I'll send Tom and Cory to meet you. At the same time, I'll coordinate with Jack and get the FBI in on this. That'll keep Krustas from deciding to do something stupid to keep this under wraps."

Jude tried to keep his breathing steady, but the idea of Sabrina facing death dropped him to his knees.

Bart pulled him up by his shoulders, getting into his face. "Pull it together, man. You gotta have your shit tight…for Sabrina's sake."

Giving himself a mental slap, Jude nodded as they ran back out of the house. Jude did not hesitate to jump into Bart's SUV. *I'm in no fuckin' position to be driving.* Once more, Bart peeled away, this time heading toward Norfolk.

Cecil had driven to the waterfront, his mind working furiously. The turn of events had him sweating but he was sure his backup plan would work. *And how fortuitous that the accommodating Ms. Taggart came back to check on the old lady.*

Sabrina looked out of the window from her position in the back seat. The evening sun was disappearing over the horizon and the shadows around the warehouses were ominous. Cecil parked next to a large building and as her eyes glanced around for possible help, she noted Krustas Inc. on a large sign. Licking her lips nervously, her attention jerked back to him as he got out of the vehicle.

Pulling her out of the car, he had hold of her arm and jerked her forward. Her hands, still taped behind her back, caused her shoulders to scream in pain. Sucking in a deep breath, she glanced around at the men working in the large space moving crates around with loaders. They gave cursory glances her way, but all continued about their business.

Sabrina tried to be brave, but her jello legs had other plans. Locking her shaking knees into place was the only way she could be sure that she would not end up on the warehouse floor in a puddle.

"Nastelli!"

Hearing a shout to her left, she jerked her head toward the sound at the same time Cecil slung her whole body around causing her to fall toward him as she lost her balance. His fingers dug into her upper arm as he righted her body with a growl.

Seeing three men approach, she eyed them warily. All three in dark suits, two were bulky men straight from a mob movie. Their faces hard, but impassive. The one in the middle was taller. Leaner. And his expression? Definitely not happy.

Stopping right in front of them, she noted the man in the middle barely glanced her way. *Is that a good sign or a bad sign,* she wondered.

"I brought—"

"Shut the fuck up, you moron," the man said, his smooth voice belying the growl underneath.

Turning on his heel, he began to walk away while the two bulky sidekicks flanked her and Cecil. He continued to jerk her arm although she was walking beside him. When the two men stopped suddenly, so did Cecil causing her to slam once more into him. Wincing in pain, she wanted to rail against his unnecessary hold on her. *Where the hell does he think I'm going to go?*

She watched as one of the silent goons dropped his eyes to Cecil's grip on her arm and then back up to his face, and immediately felt her injured arm released. Before she could process the silent communications, they were once again walking toward the taller man who was ascending stairs on the side of the warehouse. Glancing upward, she saw a room above with glass windows overlooking the work area. Reaching the bottom of the stairs in a silent formation, one bruiser led the way followed by her, Cecil behind and then the other hulk bringing up the rear.

With each step, her knees continued to knock as her breath came in pants. Forcing herself to breathe deeply, she fought the panic rising with each step. At the top of the stairs, there was only one way to go—following the lean man straight into the room.

"She's stopped moving," Luke reported over the phone to Jude. Rattling off the location, he continued to fill him in on the surrounding area. Disconnecting with him, Jude quickly relayed the information to Jared's group.

"Don't worry," Jared said. "You concentrate on what you're doing. I'm coordinating with Jack and my men. When you get there, do not go in with guns blazing. Tom and Cory will work with you and Bart."

As hard as it was for Jude to agree, he did. Closing his eyes for a moment, he mentally chanted. *Gather the intel. Plan the mission. Execute the mission.* He had done that as a SEAL and would need to do it once more if he wanted Sabrina safe. *But this time it's so fuckin' hard!*

Relaying that they needed to wait to rendezvous with Tom and Cory, he knew Bart did not like it any more than he did. But both men would follow orders— to not do so might cost Sabrina her life.

Entering the warehouse office, Sabrina was escorted to the middle of the room. A quick glance showed the interior did not look like a mob space. At least not what she imagined from movies. The furniture was grey metal, egalitarian. A desk, chairs, conference table, filing cabinets. But what sat behind the desk matched her imaginations perfectly. An older man, heavy-set, with a square jaw and eyes that did not appear to miss anything. *Mr. Krustas.* She recognized his face from the news. Her mind racing, she tried to remember what she read. *He was charged but later cleared by the Feds, but several members of his family had been sent to prison for extortion, illegal smuggling, and racketeering.*

The leaner man walked to stand beside the seated gentleman, both glaring at Cecil with only cursory looks in her direction.

Cecil opened his mouth to speak but was immediately silenced by a simple raised hand from the older man, who finally gave his attention to her. With a nod to the goon at her side, she saw the flash of a knife but before she could do more than gasp, the tape around her wrists was sliced, freeing her arms.

Bringing them to the front, she rubbed her hands together to get the circulation moving, wincing as they tingled.

"Please have a seat," the gentleman offered, nodding to the chair that was closest to her. She immediately sat, knowing she needed to keep her wits and definitely not wanting to piss him off. At least for now, he did not appear to be angry with her.

"What the hell were you thinking to bring this woman to our door?" he asked. Not raising his voice, its icy coldness was fierce all the same. Before Cecil could open his mouth, he continued. "And I had better like your answer."

She sat as still as possible but could not help but move her eyes toward the left where Cecil stood. His earlier bravado was slipping, if wiping his hands on his expensive pants was any indication.

"She's collateral," Cecil began. "I can't get what I owe you right now, but I will and—"

Cecil halted once more with a raised hand from Mr. Krustas. She saw his eyes jerk toward her and then off to the side. The man, standing on her right, placed his hand gently on her arm and assisted her to stand, before ushering her to the side of the room toward another door. Eyes wide in panic, she looked over at Mr. Krustas.

"My apologies, Ms. Taggart. I will have Frank escort you to another, more comfortable, room where you may find some refreshments while I deal with Mr. Nastelli."

Barely able to nod, she allowed herself to stumble

into the next room. Inside, she was amazed. Dark paneled walls met maroon carpet. The desk in this room was heavy oak, with matching chairs. A credenza sat behind the desk, crystal decanters centered along with silver picture frames holding what she assumed were family photographs.

The man identified as Frank spoke for the first time. "You may make yourself at home here, Miss. There's water and juice in the refrigerator," he said, nodding toward the wall. "A bathroom is through that door. There is no other exit so, please do not attempt to leave."

Wanting to move away from him she immediately walked to the bathroom, shutting and locking the door. Placing her hands on the sink, she bowed her head as she steadied her breathing. Finally, she looked into the mirror seeing her pale complexion. As her gaze drifted down to the sparkle around her neck, she focused on the St. Jude pendant. Patron Saint of the impossible. *The tracer is attached! Please, Jude, find me here.*

Using the facilities, she washed her hands before tidying her hair. Steeling herself with a deep breath, she let it out slowly before re-entering the luxurious office. She was hoping that Frank would have left in her absence, but no such luck. He was standing next to the office door, his bulk taking up most of the doorframe with his arms crossed in front of his chest. Walking over to the mini-frig, she retrieved a bottle of water before moving to one of the comfortable chairs.

He offered a head jerk in acknowledgment of her acquiescence before exiting the room, the click of the lock resounding in the quiet space. Jumping from her chair, she immediately rushed over, placing her ear against the door. Nothing. The heavy, wooden door was too thick. *Damn!*

Glancing around, her eyes landed on the crystal glasses on the credenza. Scurrying around the desk, she snagged one before hustling back to the door. Placing the glass against the door and her ear against the glass, she heard the voices clearly. Grinning, she remembered the times she, Bart, and the other cousins could get creative in their cops and robbers games as children. *Bart was the one who taught me the oldest listening device in the world. And it works!*

"She's worth more than I owe you," Cecil was saying.

"You cannot possibly be so stupid to think that I can ransom off a young woman from a well-known family to get the money that you owe me," Mr. Krustas roared.

"No one knows where we are. I didn't say anything in front of the old woman. My plan was perfect. It's always worked before. I got the money, but found out the bitch was on to me and put a hold on the bank accounts. But you can use her. You know...a pretty girl..."

A gasp escaped before she could stop it, but she knew the door was too thick for them to hear her. *Oh, my God. What are they planning?* She heard a whine in Cecil's voice that had not been present before. An eerie quiet followed and, strain as she might, she could hear nothing. No words. No movement.

Bart came to a sudden stop down the road from the warehouses on the bay, dusk already settling over the waterfront. Jude, recognizing Tom and Cory, jumped out before Bart cut the engine, racing over to them,

"Is she here?" he asked, his voice unable to mask his concern.

Tom nodded, "Yeah, Jared got confirmation that she's in the number 205 warehouse."

Jude turned suddenly, ready to run in, but Cory's hand on his arm stopped him.

"No, man," Cory said. "We gotta play this carefully."

Jude rounded on him, his expression a mixture of incredulity and rage. "What the fuck does that mean?"

Coming up behind him, Bart's vibes were equally as angry.

Tom and Cory shared a quick glance and then Cory continued, "The warehouse is owned by Russian mob boss, Ivan Krustas. Last year, some of his organization was busted for—"

"I know, I know," Jude interrupted. "Get to the fuckin' point before they kill Sabrina."

Tom growled, "You gotta trust Jared. He's worked with the Feds on this and Krustas has to be handled just right or years of investigation could come crashing down."

"I don't give a fuck about some goddamn investigation!" both Jude and Bart yelled at the same time.

"We're goin' in," Tom said, "but not guns blazing. We gotta go slow and careful or we'll make this a lot worse...for Sabrina."

At the mention of her name, Jude calmed slightly. *At least they're thinking of her as well.* "Why?" he demanded.

"Old man Krustas turned some evidence over to the Feds, clearing his name in front of the public and keeping his legitimate businesses from being dragged down with his nephew's illegal end of the business. He's careful to funnel what he does through a lot of channels to keep his name out. The Feds want to catch him but treat him with kid gloves until they can get what they want on the nephew. He's got no reason to hurt Sabrina right now, so we go in slow and easy."

Sucking in a deep breath, he looked to the side at Bart, who was doing the same. Before either man could speak, Tom said, "We go in, but trust in Jared. Just like when you were a SEAL. Execute the mission. He knows what he's talking about."

Trust? With Sabrina's life? Digging deep, he pulled upon all of his SEAL training and nodded. "I'm ready," he acknowledged. "Let's go."

Sabrina continued to strain, attempting to listen to the conversation.

"The money you owe me is legitimate. I will not allow a little shit-stain like yourself to taint what I am trying to do here."

"What you're trying to do?" Cecil's voice rose with each word. "You're up to your eyeballs in extortion—umph."

She heard the sound of flesh hitting flesh and could

only imagine the next sound was Cecil crumpling to the floor. Clutching her stomach, she willed it not to revolt. She sucked in a deep breath in an attempt to keep from throwing up...or fainting.

"Get him out of here," Mr. Krustas ordered. "Permanently."

"No, no..." Cecil's pleas carried through the listening glass she had pressed to her ear.

"What about the girl?" another man's voice asked, presumably from the leaner man who had initially met them in the warehouse. *Oh God, if they're going to kill Cecil, why would they keep me alive?* She could hear the sound of a chair scraping against the floor and imagined that Mr. Krustas was standing from behind his desk.

Flying across the carpet, she placed the glass back on the credenza with shaking hands, trying to remember its exact location so that no one would be the wiser. Skirting around the desk, she plopped back down into the chair that Frank had last seen her in.

Forcing her breathing to even, she clasped her hands together in an attempt to quell the shaking. The door opened, the parade of men filing into the room. Mr. Krustas, the lean man, and Frank. The other bruiser was not with them, presumedly to cart off Cecil.

She watched warily as Mr. Krustas glided across the carpet and settled into the elegant chair behind the desk. He sat, quietly observing her, saying nothing. Silence reigned for a moment before he spoke.

"You are unusually quiet and composed for a woman."

Surprised, she cocked her head to the side, asking, "For a woman?"

He chuckled before explaining, "It is my observation that women often do not know when to keep their mouths shut and especially in a trying and confusing situation. I would have not been surprised to find you weeping and begging."

Terrified, but equally irritated, she replied, "Then you are undoubtedly not associating with the right women."

Throwing his head back, he roared with laughter as his hand slapped down on the desk. Finally agreeing, he said, "You may be right, Ms. Taggart." As his mirth slowed, he said, "You have surmised that Mr. Nastelli owed money to me. It was a legitimate loan, I assure you. Nothing untoward, but he is unable to pay and, unfortunately, made an error in judgment that by bringing you to me, I would somehow become involved with his scheme."

"And that scheme was..." she prompted.

"He was giving you to me and supposedly I was to ransom you back to your grandmother who would pay an exorbitant fee to have you back unharmed."

Glancing at the unsmiling face of the lean man standing once more to Mr. Krustas' left, she cocked her head to the side. "I may not know much about criminal activities, but that does not sound like a very viable plan."

Chuckling again, Mr. Krustas looked up at the man next to him and repeated, "Not a viable plan. I like Ms.

Taggart very much. Meeting her is the only thing out of this fucked up situation that has been worthwhile."

"Glad I could amuse," she said, anger overriding fear. "May I be so bold as to ask what you are going to do with me?"

He turned his steely gaze back to hers. "Now, my dear. We wait."

As soon as Jude reached the opening to the warehouse with Bart, Cory, and Rick, he stopped quickly, seeing a man waiting for them at the entrance. Jared Rogers. The owner of a security business and the boss of Tom and Cory. *What's he doing here?*

Before he could ask, Jared nodded at the group and said, "Gentlemen. Follow me."

Jude and Bart shared an incredulous look, before falling into step behind him with Tom and Cory bringing up the rear. Moving to their vehicle first, they quickly suited up. Jude pulled on the Kevlar vest, liking the feel of familiar weight. He and Bart had already armed themselves with what Bart had with him, but quickly added a Glock G41 to his arsenal. As the men readied themselves, they all turned to Jared for instructions, who with a nod led them forward.

Moving tactically, the group separated. Jared, Cory, and Bart circled around toward the left leaving Tom and Jude moving to the right. The warehouse appeared empty at first glance, but it did not take the group long to locate the few employees standing guard.

Creating a diversion, Cory drew the attention of the two men nearest the wooden crates on the side allowing Jared and Bart to subdue them. With the use of zip-ties, they quickly immobilized the men with their hands behind their backs and gags in their mouths.

Jude and Tom came to the guard at the bottom of the stairs, whose attention was diverted to the scuffle from the side of the warehouse. Throwing his arm around the beefy man's neck, Jude immobilized him as well, tossing him to the ground. With a grin, Jude kneed him in the back, using his zip-ties to subdue him as well.

The five men met at the stairs, Jared nodding to Cory and Tom to stand guard, before jerking his head to Jude and Bart to follow him. Ascending a metal stair-case on the side, they entered a modest office. Standing outside of a door across the room was a large man, arms across his chest. Nodding to Jared, he moved to the side after knocking once on the door before opening it.

Jared motioned for Jude to precede him and with a questioning glance, he walked into the next room, immediately noting its elegance compared to the room he just passed through. Then his eyes landed on the woman, sitting stiff-backed in the chair in front of the desk, a second before she threw herself at him.

"Jude!" she screamed, flying into his arms. He easily hoisted her up as she wrapped her body around his. He could feel her body quivering and tried to comfort her with one hand behind her head and the other holding her tightly against his chest.

"Ah, young love. How sweet."

Jude heard the droll words coming from the man sitting behind the desk. "Someone better tell me what the fuck is going on," he growled.

"Jared," Mr. Krustas nodded toward him as he walked in.

"Ivan," Jared responded in acknowledgment.

Jude turned quickly toward Jared, his eyes demanding an explanation.

Jared walked over as Jude gently set Sabrina on her feet, steadying her with his body. "You okay?"

She nodded before managing to say, "Yes, but—"

Bart stalked over, stopping next to Jude, placing his hand protectively on his cousin's shoulder. "Jared? What the fuck is going on?"

"As soon as I heard that Nastelli was bringing her here, I placed a call. Mr. Krustas has been…um… assisting my group and, in turn, the Feds in cleaning up some of his family's nefarious activities. I simply informed him that a young woman was being brought to him and it would behoove him to make sure she was safe until we could come."

"And I was more than glad to do so," Mr. Krustas added.

Sabrina licked her lips nervously. "So…um, you… work for the…um…good guys?"

Jared chuckled as he shook his head. Mr. Krustas actually appeared embarrassed at her question.

"Ah, I wouldn't exactly put it that way, Ms. Taggart. I

admit that Mr. Nastelli did owe me quite a bit of money and I expected to be paid back. With interest," he added, pinning her with a knowing gaze. Before she could reply, he continued. "But Mr. Rogers is correct. I have worked with his group. I do not care for human trafficking and working for the...good guys, as you say... has not been a problem. And," he spread his hands out wide, "if it keeps the authorities out of my business... well...all the better."

"But...what about Mr. Nastelli? We need to turn him over to the police. He didn't get my grandmother's money, but he's a crook! We need to—"

"He will not bother you anymore," he assured.

"But, but—"

"He will not bother anyone anymore. His psychic days are *over,*" Mr. Krustas emphasized, lifting one eyebrow at her. His tone implied that no more questions would be acceptable.

Biting her lip she turned to look at Jude, but saw his hard expression. She then turned to look into Jared's face, but a quick shake of his head had her quietly leaning back against Jude's strong embrace.

As they began to file out of the room, she glanced back at Mr. Krustas who had risen from his desk and called out her name.

"It was a pleasure to meet you, Ms. Taggart. I doubt ourn paths will ever cross again, but if you should ever need something—"

"She'll have me," Jude interjected, pulling her gently into his embrace.

Nodding, the older man smiled. "As it should be," he replied just before Frank closed the door.

Two hours later, the group sat in Arlene's family room, the men sprawled on her comfortable sofas and chairs. Jude sat with Sabrina in his lap, not wanting to let her out of his arms. Bart fussed over his grandmother, but she insisted that she was fine and wanted to hear all about the events after Sabrina had been taken from her house.

Sabrina described the trip to the warehouse and her fears once they were there. She explained how she listened to the conversation on the other side of the door using the glass. Jared, Cory, and Tom laughed at her ingenuity while Bart, remembering their games as children, rolled his eyes and Jude squeezed her even tighter.

They all sobered as she described what she had heard near the end of the conversation with Cecil. "I don't know what they planned, but Cecil kept intimating that Krustas would want me for some reason."

Jared replied, "The other Krustas perhaps, but that was a major blunder of Nastelli. Krustas' nephew, Sergio, dealt in human trafficking and Nastelli must have thought that if he could get you to them, then your value as a woman would cover his debt."

"But what I don't understand is why you didn't call the police, Jared?" Sabrina prodded.

Taking a deep breath, he said, "There're things that I can't tell you, but here's what I can. Last year, Ivan Krustas learned that one of his nephews was deeply involved in human trafficking and the Feds were looking to bust not only that enterprise, but anything else even closely related to the Krustas empire. Ivan stood to lose everything. He began working with the FBI and the agreement was that he would give up his nephew and all of that sordid affair for a certain amount of leniency as he worked his legitimate businesses."

Sabrina nodded slowly, "Okay, I get that. But how did Cecil get involved?"

Cory took up the explanation, saying, "About ten years ago, he developed the mystical, psychic angle and used it on some unsuspecting wealthy widows from as far north as New York and all the way down to Florida. We even believe that he worked the mid-west in Chicago and Denver as well. Never staying in one place too long, he learned how to change his identity and cover his tracks."

"I knew that goddamn fortune-telling, psychic, mumbo-jumbo asshole was a total phony. Christ, I can't stand preying on innocents by using that voodoo shit," Bart exclaimed. "If I can't see it, touch it, feel it, then it's not real!"

"And Nastelli's involvement with Ivan?" Jude asked.

Tom said, "As best as we can tell, it simply came down to Nastelli's luck running out. He got into the Hampton Roads area right after his investments took a hit and borrowed money to get started on his scams here. He figured he would make plenty to pay Ivan back and live a rich life until he needed to score more some-where else."

"He didn't count on anything going wrong, did he?" Sabrina asked.

"Most scammers don't think they'll get caught."

"Jared?" Sabrina said softly, an underlying current of fear running through her voice. "I heard...I mean...Cecil—"

"He's fine, Sabrina."

Wide-eyed, she asked, "He didn't get whacked by Krustas? He's not swimming with the fishes?" The others chuckled as she blushed. "Well, you know what I mean," she said.

"No, what you heard was real. They let him think that he was going to get...*whacked*, as you say. In actual-ity, the FBI were downstairs and Krustas turned him over to them. It's all part of Ivan's attempt to appear legitimate."

"Oh, thank God. I hated what he did, but..." her words drifted off as Jude gave her a reassuring hug.

Arlene gasped, saying, "And he would have gotten away with it if you all hadn't been watching out for me." Dropping her head, she shook her head sadly. "There's no fool like an old fool."

Sabrina jumped from Jude's lap, rushing over to kneel in front of her grandmother. "No, Nonnie. You're no fool. He was slick. He was smart. He knew what to say to make you hope."

Arlene looked up, heaving first a sigh and then a deep cleansing breath. "You were right the other day, Sabrina. My John is dead. He can't reveal anything else to us now, but he gave us a lifetime of lessons to learn from."

Sabrina kissed her grandmother's soft cheek before walking back into Jude's strong embrace.

Jared looked over at Jude, saying, "You did a great job with this investigation. My offer still stands, you know. You want a job with me, you've got one."

Jude noticed Bart's gaze land on him, an intense expression on his face. Jude smiled as he replied, "Thanks, Jared. That means more to me than you can know, but...well, I've decided I need a change in scenery. One not so close to a Naval base. I'm taking Jack up on his offer to work with his company."

Bart gave a whoop, leaning over to fist-bump Jude. "Welcome to the Saints, bro!"

Jared laughed and added, "Who knows? We may be working together sometime in the future."

The group settled, each to their own thoughts for a minute before Jude spoke again. "You know, I've realized that Nastelli did reveal something to me through all of this." He noticed the questioning gazes from everyone in the room but focused on the upturned face of the beautiful woman in his arms.

"What did he reveal?" she asked softly.

"That as long as a man has family and friends, then he has all he needs in life. And you, Sabrina," he said, lifting his hand to cup her silken cheek, "have been my best friend. And now I want you to be my family."

She gasped just before he placed a sweet kiss on her lips. As he leaned back she began to question him but he interrupted.

"Yeah, babe. I want you to be my wife. Will you marry me?"

With shouts coming from everyone in the room, including Arlene, the two lovers kissed. Jude poured his love into this kiss...one of friendship...one of love...one of forever.

13

Three months later

Shoving the last box into the large U-haul, Jude looked up toward Sabrina's apartment building to watch her walk down the steps carrying...*another container?* Turning to glance back into the packed trailer he said, "Babe, I don't know where we're gonna put that!"

Grinning, she replied, "Don't worry. It's for our helpers!"

That news sent several men heading her way. Cory and Tom immediately reached her side, the scent of chocolate chip cookies drifting from the plastic tub she held. "Guys, these are for you since you helped us so much getting everything loaded."

The men dove into the goodies, moaning in grati-tude. "Damn, these are good," Cory enthused.

Jude strolled over, throwing a possessive arm

around Sabrina kissing the top of her head. "You once said I was a lucky fuck to have this girl. Now you really know how lucky," he joked.

The friends stood for a few minutes letting the afternoon breeze cool their bodies before the men checked the trailer once more and securing the back. Loaded with both Jude's possessions and hers as well, they were ready to leave.

The men offered her cheek kisses and hugs goodbye before moving over to Jude and shaking his hand.

"You've got a great girl and a great new job, but don't forget your old friends," Cory said, pulling Jude into a man hug.

Tom moved over, offering the same advice. "We're always here if you need us," he added.

With goodbyes finally over, Jude assisted Sabrina into his SUV and they pulled out of the parking lot. Hearing her sigh, he glanced over. "You okay, babe? Is it leaving Arlene?"

"No, no. Nonnie was tearful but knew that this was a great opportunity for both of us. And she'll be fine. It seems like after the Cecil fiasco, she has snapped back into the take-charge woman that we knew before granddad passed away."

"I hate that for her, but sometimes the best life-lessons come from the hardest things to deal with."

"Oohh, sage advice," she giggled. "I take it you talk from experience?"

By now they were well on their way toward the central part of Virginia, a new rental house waiting for them. Arlene had wanted them to marry first but they were anxious to begin their new jobs so decided to move first and then plan a wedding.

"Yeah," he answered. "I'd say I learned it the hard way. I don't know if it was the Patron Saint of lost causes, but I certainly was one. You didn't give up on me and now I promise to you that I'll never give up on us."

With the highway in front of them and the setting sun behind them, she leaned over kissing his cheek. Linking her hand with his, she settled back into her seat, the future they always wanted lying before them.

Ready for Bart's story? Click here!
Seeing Love

Don't miss any news about new releases! Sign up for my Newsletter

ALSO BY MARYANN JORDAN

Don't miss other Maryann Jordan books!

Lots more Baytown stories to enjoy and more to come!

Baytown Boys (small town, military romantic suspense)

Coming Home

Just One More Chance

Clues of the Heart

Finding Peace

Picking Up the Pieces

Sunset Flames

Waiting for Sunrise

Hear My Heart

Guarding Your Heart

Sweet Rose

Our Time

Count On Me

Shielding You

To Love Someone

Sea Glass Hearts

For all of Miss Ethel's boys:

Heroes at Heart (Military Romance)

Zander

Rafe

Cael

Jaxon

Jayden

Asher

Zeke

Cas

Lighthouse Security Investigations

Mace

Rank

Walker

Drew

Blake

Tate

Levi

Clay

Cobb

Hope City (romantic suspense series co-developed

with Kris Michaels

Brock book 1

Sean book 2

Carter book 3

Brody book 4

Kyle book 5

Ryker book 6

Rory book 7

Killian book 8

Torin book 9

Saints Protection & Investigations

(an elite group, assigned to the cases no one else wants...or can solve)

Serial Love

Healing Love

Revealing Love

Seeing Love

Honor Love

Sacrifice Love

Protecting Love

Remember Love

Discover Love

Surviving Love

Celebrating Love

Searching Love

Follow the exciting spin-off series:

Alvarez Security (military romantic suspense)

Gabe

Tony

Vinny

Jobe

SEALs

Thin Ice (Sleeper SEAL)

SEAL Together (Silver SEAL)

Undercover Groom (Hot SEAL)

Also for a Hope City Crossover Novel / Hot SEAL...

A Forever Dad by Maryann Jordan

Letters From Home (military romance)

Class of Love

Freedom of Love

Bond of Love

The Love's Series (detectives)

Love's Taming

Love's Tempting

Love's Trusting

The Fairfield Series (small town detectives)

Emma's Home

Laurie's Time

Carol's Image

Fireworks Over Fairfield

Please take the time to leave a review of this book. Feel free to contact me, especially if you enjoyed my book. I love to hear from readers!

Facebook

Email

Website

ABOUT THE AUTHOR

I am an avid reader of romance novels, often joking that I cut my teeth on the historical romances. I have been reading and reviewing for years. In 2013, I finally gave into the characters in my head, screaming for their story to be told. From these musings, my first novel, Emma's Home, The Fairfield Series was born.

I was a high school counselor having worked in education for thirty years. I live in Virginia, having also lived in four states and two foreign countries. I have been married to a wonderfully patient man for thirty-five years. When writing, my dog or one of my four cats can generally be found in the same room if not on my lap.

Please take the time to leave a review of this book. Feel free to contact me, especially if you enjoyed my book. I love to hear from readers!

Facebook
Email
Website

Made in the USA
Las Vegas, NV
11 November 2021

34200640R00090